Sońka

Ignacy Karpowicz

SOŃKA

Translated from the Polish by Maya Zakrzewska-Pim

DALKEY ARCHIVE PRESS

Originally published in Polish as *Sońka* by Wydawnictwo Literackie in 2014.

Copyright © 2014 by Ignacy Karpowicz
Translation copyright © 2018 by Maya Zakrzewska-Pim
First Dalkey Archive edition, 2018.

Library of Congress Cataloging-in-Publication Data
Names: Karpowicz, Ignacy, author. | Zakrzewska-Pim, Maya, translator.
Title: Sonka / by Ignacy Karpowicz ; translated from Polish by Maya Zakrzewska-Pim.
Other titles: Sonka. English
Description: First Dalkey Archive edition. | Victoria, TX : Dalkey Archive, 2018. | "Originally published in Polish by Wydawnictwo Literackie as Sonka in 2014" -- Verso title page.
Identifiers: LCCN 2017036700 | ISBN 9781628972351 (pbk. : alk. paper)
Subjects: LCSH: Young women--Poland--Fiction. | Germany. Heer--Officers--Fiction. | World War, 1939-1945--Fiction. | Poland--Fiction. | GSAFD: War stories. g | Love stories. g
Classification: LCC PG7211.A765 S6613 2018 | DDC 891.8/538--dc23
LC record available at https://lccn.loc.gov/2017036700

www.dalkeyarchive.com
Victoria, TX / McLean, IL / Dublin

Co-funded by the Creative Europe Programme of the European Union

Dalkey Archive Press publications are, in part, made possible through the support of the University of Houston-Victoria and its programs in creative writing, publishing, and translation.

Printed on permanent/durable acid-free paper.

For good people

ONCE UPON A TIME—that's how Sonia began the sentences which didn't feature cows, chickens and pigs, holidays, bread and taxes, harvests, digging and hail; that's how she began the sentences that got stuck somewhere in the throat, that paused on the smooth, toothless gums, only to slip back down into the body: into the lungs, heart, and dust, to form little balls among the old, used organs. But sometimes, after this "once upon a time," sometimes the words overcame the obstacles, breaking through the layer of meat and time, sounding out fully before finally being reabsorbed into the body: they traveled to the brain via the ears, and searched for a place there, they waited, until dreams loosened events and problems—then, not for the first time, the words were dreamed into a story, both the good and the bad, depending on one's perspective, depending on the moment of awakening and the destinations never reached.

Ten, thirty, maybe fifty years have passed, but for Sonia, for the last twenty, forty, or sixty years the once-upon-a-time has been equally distant. And after this "once" and that "time," after them came the same time, the time when Sońka, still very young, lived and felt so much that afterward she didn't live or feel at all. Then, she waved her hand, all the safety locks burst open, just like that!

Because people aren't, she always said, composed of any lasting material, they're made of what they eat: of milk, meat and flour, of fruit, mushrooms, prosphora and salt. Especially salt. That's what gives the whole some kind of taste and shape, ensuring that people don't rot but dry up instead, until eventually all they resemble is a bone that has been exposed to rain and sun alike.

Because when a person, and especially a country woman, feels too much and lives too fast, then something sparks, and sparks some more, and then the whole installation fails: God, our *Hospadzi*[1], has no return policy, even though He often forgets to send out the handyman dressed in a cloak and skull, the one who cuts people's legs from under them with a scythe, so at least a temporary cleanliness and order can reign until the clean bright domes and a final order arrive, which will be reflected in the eyes of the saints, eyes like wells built of golden planks at the very spring of nothingness.

Sonia pulled out the skewer of the chain, at the end of which a cow stood calmly. It chewed grass and gave milk, had a calf every two years, provided meat and skin, brought in—perhaps a small, but not insignificant—income. It produced this money like the national mint, even while asleep, or when a flat cowpat shot out from under the tail like a Rorschach test. The field fed the cow, the cow, feeding the townspeople, fed Sonia. That's how this world has been arranged—some have to eat so others may eat also. Because if everybody stopped eating, Sonia would say, then the world would thin down, and if the world got too thin, then beaver fat and healers wouldn't be enough to save it.

Sonia, having pulled out the skewer, waited for the breaths to stop painfully bouncing off her ribs, and leaned heavily on the gnarled stick, like she used to lean on the pitchfork—she used to lean more heavily on that though, so heavily, like a bag of meat—she adjusted her scarf, clucked at the cow: "*Nu, Mućka, paszła.*" The patchy dairy, self-propelled and with a heavy udder, looked at Sonia with the brownest of her brown eyes, at the bottom of which grew grass, flies flew, and tiny fish swam by in the water—*kaluczki*; their use was as small as their size, but the small and useless in times of plenty become large and indispensable in times of hunger.

---

1   Until recently Podlasie, especially its rural areas, had two linguistic realities: Polish and Belarusian. These existed separately, protecting their separateness, but simultaneously they were perfectly comprehensible to each other. This era is, unfortunately and irrevocably, ending. This is why I decided to collect the Belarusian phrases and words in one place, at the end of the book, not just for clarity, but—and this is probably the more important reason—to offer the reader the chance to immerse themselves in a different, parallel linguistic world, exotic, but nevertheless familiar.

Sonia slowly began to move, she didn't even look over her shoulder: the left one for a curse, the right to undo a spell, because she knew that the cow was familiar with the road: a narrow, trodden path that fell gently down to the riverbank; there, the cow will drink two buckets of water, and the old woman will draw out of her pocket the cheapest mint. Then uphill—you have to pause at least three times for the breath to catch up with the person, because the breath, Sonia claimed, will refuse to keep up, and if a person rushes too much, he can lose it altogether, and when that happens, then even Saint Nicholas or Saint Menas won't be able to retrieve it. And once the sandy strip appears from behind the bushes, then without any anxiousness all you need is to let your legs carry you home.

The sandy road is sometimes witness to a car from Białystok or Warsaw, if the plates are to be believed, it rushes past, sending out clouds of dust to hide it from view.

And—just like in a fairy tale, when a prince passing by on a horse recognizes his destiny in a village girl, happiness, children, and the curse of a misalliance—a limousine drives by. It drives by, but eventually it stops.

The roundworm-like body of a Mercedes S, gray like an oversized beetle, stops. The cow sneezes, chewing grass that she had collected in one of her four stomachs, and shifts her weight, interested only in the flies that want to settle on her nose. Sonia tries to use her hand as a shield against the sun, a hand—now gnarled, with splinters grown in, blisters, a history of crosses—that allows her to see more. *Tfu*, thinks Sonia, *przystanuli i buduć scać.*

But there is no emptying of the bladder. Sonia made a mistake in her choice of words, though she was correct in her assessment of what would happen next, because Sonia wasn't really trying to say anything specific; just as spring follows winter, so the stopping of a car with Warsaw plates must be followed by something out of place.

The Mercedes stopped, the dust was settling, the speakers—
the front door on the driver's side opened—exploded with
music, and the urban prince revealed himself. Instead of: "I
love you, I searched, I put up fliers," instead of that, the door
just shuts and silences the music.

The dust was settling, the car's V-8 fell silent, the cow walked
along the edge of the road, and behind it—it was unclear as to
who was leading whom—Sonia, and it was most likely there
was nothing else trailing behind it: she had offered to others
what she had a long time ago, and what she didn't have, she
could neither offer nor steal. On the same side of the road, on
the same edge, the city prince stood, with a rucksack instead
of a scepter and a smile instead of a kingdom. He was wearing
shorts with a military pattern and useless pockets, a short-
sleeved shirt that was the orange of a coypu's incisors, suede
sandals which were softer than the community lady's karakul
fur coat, Wiera's from Gródek office, who drove her own car, a
Golf, to Białystok on a weekly basis, a car made in Germany,
like a nightmare which Sonia had lived through, and if the car
was at least in part of the same high quality as the war, it was
only right to envy Wiera—it will serve her for a long time and
without fail, never leaving her head or her thoughts.

All that one can do, thought an intrigued and rather nervous
Sonia, such a pretty prince, one should stand him in a big room
and dust him once a week, and dress him in gilded flounces
for the holidays, in puffs and platypuses, burn the candles and
reach for mother's ring hidden in the sock, and look at it, look,
until one's looked enough, and then—sleep.

The city youth had a name, Sonia suspected, and a position,
which Sonia could not have guessed, and he was clearly also in
a bad mood, which caused unnecessary wrinkles to form, ones
which even Lancôme and Dr. Irena Eris could not charm away.
He spent a long time groping his pockets and peering into his
rucksack, as if he had misplaced a page of advice and answers to

all the questions in the world: what to do and how to live, what to avoid and with whom, where to avoid and for how much, and most importantly—where is the bloody phone number to fucking assistance. He did not retrieve a page, however, but cigarettes in a gold-colored packet—anyone who smokes and travels the world in an airplane would know they were from duty-free—he lit one, inhaled, and coughed. *"Zdychlina"* whispered Sonia to the cow, its self-propelled movements held back over the bush as it contemplated the nature of gadflies.

The prince retrieved a cell phone, the newest model, so beautiful and shiny that it could have served to decorate the Tsarist iconostasis, to be used in the greatest need: flood, war, right-wing politicians in power—to call the boss and complain, to open up the heart and a limitless credit line of impulses: *Spasi, Hospadzi, spasi.* Except that this cell phone, although very beautiful and very gleaming in the August sunlight, didn't connect its owner with the owner of a similar device on the other side, somewhere in some real world: with cinemas, warehouses, and pizza to be ordered by calling o-eight-hundred, with the call being free, the delivery too, as long as you pay about thirty *złotych*.

Sonia knew that the city youth stopped in a hole, a hole a hundredfold worse than others, because there was no operator who covered this part of the world, no sociologist who included its inhabitants in any statistics, even the Orthodox clergyman only grudgingly appeared in his Daewoo Espero, and then only to bless quickly and mechanically, slip the envelope into his pocket, and that's it; they saw him no more than three to five times a year, because the number of Holy Days remained unchanged.

Here, at the end of nothing, in Królowe Stojło, not far from the metropolitan Słuczanka, there were only four hovels. Sonia lived in the smallest one, mice ran freely in two others because

the inhabitants had settled in their graves, and now the city heirs
appeared for the occasional weekend, though not often; it's a pity
it's not often, it's always a change, a noise to break the silence, a
life in the emptiness of this place. The fourth hovel is different:
new, erected from concrete blocks under Kwaśniewski's second
rule—beautified by plastic windows, glimmering with the glass
of broken bottles which form mosaics of flowers, waves, and
uglies; fat dwarves stand in the garden, forming a line, like in
a concentration camp, between the cabbage patch and onion
patch, following the rule that that which is beautiful must
also be disciplined. To add to all this, the balcony has a plaster
balustrade, and small columns, and a porch, and a cornice—a
clear Russian-Słuczanski baroque.

The prince put his phone away and stood still, his back
facing the road, his eyes looking out at the fields and the line
of the nearby forest. He stood and puffed on his cigarette, with
a tanned face turned toward the sun, smiling slightly. *Musi jak
durak, bez struka*, Sońka thought when she saw the smile, and it
must be added here that Sonia's opinion was shared by a circle
of influential critics of theater and literature, as well as, though
it's a different story, a few people more familiar with the gilded,
or golden, boy.

The phenomenal figure was called Igor Grycowski and he
was the loudest and most talented (this is what some wanted),
possibly the most pretentious and lacking in any feel for the
scene (this is what others wanted) theater director, younger
than the older generation, and also a writer of a story with no
tangible plot. Igor had made himself and his name known a few
years previously, when he directed the play *Odruch warunkowy*
at the Theater for the Dramatic Arts in Warsaw.

A dry storm broke after the premiere; and the more thunder,
cracking, blowouts, and hate-filled comments appeared, the
better known *Odruch warunkowy* and Grycowski himself
became. It was downhill after that, though under the hill it

all took off! Opera, libretto, Paris and New York. A further three plays and zero novels solidified the position of the substantially-younger-than-his-peers artist, mainly on the social plane but most importantly financially.

The prince, abandoning the air-conditioned interior of the Mercedes, was probably awaiting something as extraordinary as manna, such as cell reception, even a single bar, God! give it to me, give! because he didn't move a muscle when the cow and Sonia approached and reached a close proximity, one which begged for an exchange, even one like: good day, how can I walk to the closest place with cell reception. The prince, having landed not quite where he had intended, and not quite with whom he had wanted, had clearly fallen prey to some city wonderment with the landscape. He remembered something painful. The landscape resembled a landscape, everything looked as it looked, the field and the trees, and yet the entirety of nature, the river and the sky, the road and the storks, all this nature contained within it some sort of threat. He tried to decide whether it was a threat from the past, or perhaps the promise of a future one. Eventually, he gave up, made a *blip* with his car keys and locked the vehicle. He turned unexpectedly, with a violence that almost startled the cow, though she was not a cow that startled easily, and looked at Sonia's face.

And he found himself speechless, and his lips, the top and the bigger bottom one, formed an "o," because Sonia's face is a real face, faces like that aren't carved anymore, faces like that aren't encountered anymore. Sonia's face came straight from an icon; brown, hard, cracked, without meaning or lies, but also strong, with the lighter lines of wrinkles, and she must have a hell of a lot of wrinkles, plastic surgeons would have their work cut out for them; polishing, stretching, cutting, they would have enough redundant skin for at least another three faces. Because Sonia's face is simply a face: it's clear she has been through something, it's clear that she has dreamed, but most of all a face is used for what *Haspadź* intended: to listen, look, eat, wash, kiss, smell, hiccup, cry, snort.

Igor Grycowski, with his lips frozen in an "o," this sort of fairy-tale prince understood at once that before him stood a creature he had been searching for his entire life, and we don't mean the cow, though she was fine-looking and temptingly batting her long eyelashes, we don't even mean Sonia exactly, at least not the Sonia that she was in everyday life. We mean a new Sonia, undiscovered and forgotten, an exciting Sonia, whose presence Grycowski saw and felt, when the blue eye of the old woman was upon him, looking through him: at first with some fear and distaste, and then—it cleared like the sky and faded, whitened, and shone.

"*Dobry dzień*," the *babuszka* spoke, "*szto stałaso?*" she added, because the unplanned had happened to her more than once, because she had been abandoned, broken, kicked, the world doesn't change overnight and all of a sudden, and if it does change overnight and all of a sudden, then certainly not for the better.

"Good day," Igor replied, wanting to behave appropriately and with the applicable, urban-Polish language. "The car broke down unexpectedly, and I can't get through to anyone." Then he added with some embarrassment, though he wasn't sure of the reason for it: "Germany. That's where it's from," he waved his hand between the car and the sky.

Helplessness, honesty, and beauty—let's add that the third was neither objectively unexaggerated nor striking—in the youth's face spoke to Sonia so much that she spontaneously invited him for fresh milk and pointed with a stick: first at the cow's teats, then at the roof of the hovel, which is to say somewhere between the two—at an enamel mug, obligatorily chipped. The prince nodded: "With pleasure, thank you." He let the cow and the hobbling Sonia pass, and stubbed out his cigarette butt. He trudged in the direction of the homestead, lost in growing surprise.

The gate was barely hanging on rusted hinges, fastened at an angle and overgrown with moss: like in Baba Yaga's homestead, the sister of the ugly one, who removed the pretty and new beyond her field of vision. Igor's eyes slid over the poor yard, over the blue *kastruchy* on the wooden boards, the pots showing holes in the soot-darkened bottoms thinned by fire, over the talkative group of chickens, the molted cat which slept on the doorstep, over the sticks, brooms, pitchforks, and rakes. Passing the gate, entering Sonia's domain, Igor armed himself with a magic wand to—mentally at first, for practice—change his host's life.

And he waved the wand: the sun disappeared, the whispers from the audience quieted, the opening of the play was about to begin, the main light reveals a humped figure in the darkness. "Once upon a time," Sonia says, while the gathering gives in to her voice, gazes at her face as her story plucks them from the parentheses of time, and then a standing ovation (Igor shyly stands beside the old actress, bows his head toward the tips of his shoes with a rather too-photogenic modesty); the applause lasts at least a quarter of an hour, the women faint, the men aren't ashamed to wipe a tear from their eyes and cheeks. Success.

The cow moves from hoof to hoof toward the barn, Igor sits down on a bench, Sonia has to lay out straw, milk the cow, strain the milk, pour it into the milk can, push it in front of the house onto the bench, where it will be picked up by the milkmen, which is why she gratefully looks at the boy who's collapsed like a pair of rabbit ears: he's not just pretty, but thoughtful, she thinks. Sonia is very happy, she doesn't understand where this happiness has come from, it must be noted that she hasn't felt such happiness in a long time, a very long time.

And when Sonia, before the debut on the stage, plays her only mastered role: she moves busily in the barn, paints white streaks of milk on the bucket walls, moans and curses at the cow in a friendly way (*Mućka, nastupisa, bladzina*), then Igor focuses on himself, and specifically: on his nothingness, which he hasn't yet managed to transform into a happy family with his magic wand, into popular values, into respectable morality, or into confidence that there is an afterlife.

Firstly, Igor Grycowski suffers, he suffers as deeply as a cave is deep, as widely as the ocean is wide, his ego is huge, after all. If he wanted to commit suicide, he could climb his ego and jump from its top. Secondly, he doesn't see the point in anything. He suffers from creative impotence, or the other— immanence. He sees no point to the world, no goal in his life, despite having applied methods of enhancement: drugs, porn, and philosophical literature.

Suddenly a detail, a memory, a crumb, a piece of garbage: he smiles, and withdraws another cigarette from its packet.

Sonia, having finished, stood in the doorway and pulled off her wellies. "*Paczakajcie*," she said, before entering the house. The dog, graying and old, cuddled up to Igor's feet; it begged, stank, gothic silver letters shone on its collar. With some difficulty, disgusted by the dog and the fleas, by bacteria and germs, and the dog's old age, Igor put together the word: Borbus.

"Borbus," he enunciated quietly, while the dog lifted its eyes toward him, amber eyes, almost honey-colored, with pupils of long-gone memories drowning in the tree sap.

In fairy tales animals aren't just animals, they are beings a bit below humans, but at the same time much more transparent than humans in their actions. The dog lay on its back, and now Igor realizes that Borbus is a bitch.

I am Borbus, the twelfth dog of this name, my lineage can be traced back to Borbus the First, known as Aryan, to the huge German shepherd which thrice saved my mistress's life. Once he chased off wolves which approached the window, once he followed his nose to where potatoes were hidden for winter, once he distracted soldiers—bullets meant for Sonia killed Borbus the First, my ancestor, and now I, Borbus the Twelfth, also called the Last, look after my mistress, Sonia the White. I had no pups and my line is dying out, just as Sonia's line is dying out, she does not have pups either, we will die out together, I say, Borbus the Twelfth and the Last; and the angels will step down and bow their radiant heads to my mistress, and I will step with her into the sands of nothingness and I will bark for the worship of the absent Father. Hallelujah. Woof, woof.

Igor felt faint. He hadn't had lunch today, and his breakfast consisted of dietary supplements in the form of two lines of cocaine with an undoubtedly low caloric value. An eyelid hid the bitch's eye from him, no longer amber, but bright yellow, like fresh scrambled eggs, a duck's egg, and ribbons on the flags of a procession. I am in a fairy tale, he thought, in a fairy tale about life. A life following any other conventions would be unbearable. Maybe I will be saved after all, or at least substantially edited?

Before he was saved, and later executed, because there can be no other end, the heat from the cigarette burned his fingers, the dog jumped to its feet, sadly wagged its tail, and trudged toward its doghouse. Sonia appeared in the door.

"*Chadzi na małako, chadzi,*" she said.

Igor rose from the bench. He took off his felt sandals before the threshold—they were so out of place, with a price tag higher than the annual price of rent. He realized that he hadn't had friends in years who would be visited barefoot; everyone earns too much. He entered the cool, dark entrance hall, which smelled of fermented milk, pork fat and onions, hay, marinated cabbage and smoke, sweat, soap suds and grain. There was the kitchen after the next threshold: a painted blue dresser, a simple table, a worn-out plastic tablecloth with flowers, two chairs, a huge masonry heater with a *leżajka*, a low table with a bucket of water, wooden floorboards painted brown, an icon in the right corner, two tapestries on the whitened walls in a language only half-known to Sonia, and frankly she was indifferent to it: "Fresh water for health" and "When the housewife cooks, everyone enjoys the food."

"You don't have any sewage system installed?" he asked.

"*Pa szto?*" she replied. "So that my house rots from the sink in the kitchen? To sleep under one roof with my own shit?"

When Igor stepped over the threshold to the kitchen, Sonia glanced at the unexpected guest and understood in a flash that she had been looking out for this guest for many years, for a long time, since the end of the war, which turned out to be the end of her life. The war destroyed her, but it didn't break her. She realized that she was looking not at a prince, but at an angel of death; that she would be able to tell her story, present her actions for judgment. She understood that with her final word, the small flickering light within her would die—and they talked late into the night, and then they didn't live happily ever after; other than in memory. Sonia understood why she had been so very happy; because here a real angel had entered her home, not one bought and prayed for from an Orthodox church, the etymology of the angel, messenger, *malak*, the final word.

She gestured toward the chair, the prince sat down without a word, and she, happily, poured the milk into the enamel mug, placed *ahłatki* on the table, *pyszki*, that is, flat flour pies fried that morning, she retrieved her greatest treasure from the dresser, reserved for the most important guests, such as *baciuszka* or God: a metal box with chocolates.

She bought the box three years ago, in the shape of a red heart, with a beautiful, golden caption: E. Wedel. She had eyed the box for about half a year before that, it was so wonderful, so expensive and unattainable. She looked at it and couldn't imagine the red heart on her own dresser, on the knitted serviette, next to the teeth. She dreamed of it, it appeared in her dreams at night, she drooled onto the pillow—until, one day, she asked for the chocolates. The shop attendant, daughter to Irka from Mieleszki, was baffled: "*Wy, Sońka, zdurnieli,*" she said. "Maybe I've lost my mind," Sońka agreed, "but I'm not getting any younger, I simply can, I have pension documents from the doctor, and you should be ashamed."

Sonia tore the foil off the heart so she could open it: first the red one with the golden caption and the chocolates, then the one that was dry as an acorn and dumb as a swan in between the ribs and with no caption from its creators. Sonia remembered her mother as clearly as a gouged-out eye. Her mother died in childbirth, and it was a time when the female body knew no rest; just as it had to give birth to fields every year; from the godly egg a new person grew, made their way into the world, and usually soon after let themselves be taken to Heaven, as long as the priest had christened, and *Boh* accepted; you never knew with them, rapacious as they both are. And they had no cars before the war, and now you need to pay for gas separately. Before the war, *Isus Chrystos* was cheaper, more available, and the *baciuszki* transport vehicle ate grass, and grass grew for free.

Igor traced circles with his foot on the multicolored, knitted *szmatnik*, he took another sip of milk, which resembled the same beverage found in cartons only in its color, because its taste was strange, the taste and smell of a warm animal rather than the sterility of chain production. He reached for a chocolate with a green frosting, probably pistachio, he thought.

"*Patom razpalu u pieczy,*" Sonia said and sat opposite her guest.

"Later, the heater," Igor corrected her in the true urban language. Igor had hidden his childhood carefully, painted it over, was ceaselessly embarrassed by it, he scrupulously forgot it, denied it, and buried it. A childhood he spent with his grandparents in a nearby village. It used to be and still is known as Wysranka, because where his grandparents and great-grandparents lived, the world ended, probably not the world overall, because there are ends of the world with palm trees, with mountains of ice, with desert sands, but this little part of the world of Podlasie found its boundary there: at the line of birches and the last hovel, which had stood since Sławoj's day, who had improved hygiene by ordering outhouses.

General Sławoj decided that in the reborn Rzeczpospolita even the ass has its inalienable and free-sitting rights: these included the right to shit in peace in a separate, wooden house—in the temple of shit, known as a "słajowka." Before this, people went into the trees on the edge of the village, in Wysranka, worshipping the rule that the ass wants shade as much as the wolf is called to the forest; and watch where you step!

"Tasty pies," the prince said with his mouth full. Sonia smiled in reply, and her smile was complete, since the teeth that had sat on the dresser had found their way into her mouth. "I'm Igor," he said, not mentioning his kingdom, Warsaw and the stage, the glass towers and princesses full of chemicals and alcohol, the audience and the emptiness more difficult to bear than the words of the critics.

I'm Igor, I've done this and that, I have such and such awards, not to mention the nominations, which also count, not here, but there—yes. I'm Igor, fans give me their phone numbers, rivals laugh and plot behind my back, and the nights are long and lit by the glow of city lights. I'm Igor, I haven't really achieved anything, everything is ash, ash is everything, everywhere, in lungs and on the nose, under eyelids and in mouths, it scratches at the throat like cigarette smoke, and that's how it'll be until the end: a single blow is enough and there won't even be a "the end."

I have an expensive apartment, antiques in the apartment, and not a speck of dust on the antiques, thanks to the Ukrainian girl who dusts everything once a week, and I'm the only object in the house untouched by her.

I'm Sonia, my bitch, Borbus the Twelfth and the Last, calls me the White, for my gray hair, the rest of which is twined into my skull. I have a cow, Mućka, a dog, some chickens, and Jozik the cat, I have no close relatives, I have no estate, I have nothing, but it doesn't matter, because I won't be able to take anything with me on the final journey: not Mućka, not Borbus, not Jozik; why would I have anything else, if what I have I can't take with me?

That's how they might speak to each other for the first time—Igor over the pies, Sonia with a carefully chosen chocolate clasped in her bony fingers; the first version was later rewritten many times, because unspoken words don't cease to be words, just as unshat shit doesn't cease to be shit. That's the nature of everything.

August '41, a million and some years ago, as if before the Deluge, once upon a time. I was young, I had two brothers, they were older than me, Witek and Janek, I had my whole life ahead of me, the hands of someone who works, small joys, hidden feelings, I liked to roll my tongue into a tube, to plait my hair. I couldn't even hate my father down to the roots. "*Dicia lubi jak w duszu, a trasi jak hruszu,*" he said, before he started to hit, I preferred to be hit than to be loved though, hitting is easier to bear than love from your own father, especially since he's only loved me since I flowered. My father lurked, waiting for me, since I was a baby. You killed my wife, now you'll pay, he said. But I would never have hurt my mother! I didn't even know her!

Even the eldest couldn't recall such an August, everything grew heavy and fertile, it seemed this growing would be limitless, as if the good God had decided to rescale the world, deciding that from that August everything would be bigger. And it was—even my head was in the clouds, because the sky had bent under the weight of the stars, so low it leaned on the shawl I had tied on the back of my neck or under my chin. That August, the sun almost never set, the river barely flowed, there were more fish and crabs in it than water. Bees walked back to their beehives, over sand and grass, heaving loads of pollen that made it impossible to take flight. Chickens laid heaps of eggs, each with two yolks and chicks. The querns worked easily and lightly, slippery in the heat. Grain and potatoes fermented within three days, and caused drunkenness in a quarter of an hour.

Life had never been so easy before: not in Prussia, or in Tsarist or Soviet Russia, or in God's Poland, the *staryki* announced. We knew that we were now Hitler Adolf's subjects, that was the gossip, that Adolf Hitler is evil embodied, evil because he hates us and our neighbors, though he also knows nothing about us, but we didn't mind, the new war gave our villages a wide berth.

And it was a time of many wars, none of which were ours. *Palaki* fought the Germans and the Russians, now the Russians and the Germans, none of that touched us though, because we aren't like them, we're nobody's, just our own, maybe further, in Białystok, but not here, maybe in Gródek, but not in Królowe Stojło. The end of the world can be characterized by the fact that war rarely reaches it, and usually in the form of bedraggled deserters, twisted rumors, and a resounding thunder on the horizon; but if it does reach us, it's in a frightening form. We were only going to experience this later.

That day, having finished my chores, I went out to the bench, alone, because my brothers were nowhere to be found, they were probably with the Gryk girls, and my father was visiting a neighbor. I consequently sat on the bench by myself, the sun plaited its rays, played gleams on the wood, and its sounds were like woodlice against pith, on the green leaves of my dress, decorated with small forget-me-nots. Because—I don't know what I was thinking—I picked out my best dress, the one to be worn to the Orthodox church, weddings, and funerals. I really don't know what I was thinking. I sat: clean and dressed up, somewhat sad and very tired, with no idea how to live my own life. My father didn't want to give me away to a decent *muszczynu*—I was needed in my mother's stead.

If father could see me now, I'd be punished, and my mother, God rest her soul, but father went to a neighbor, which meant that he wouldn't be back until night. First I felt the delicate trembling of the air: the heavy, visible layers turned wavy, they began to separate, unstick from each other like enamel from teeth, losing their clarity. The air looked duller. Then—I say then, though it was many, many years ago—then, small columns of dust rose from the sandy road, staying in the air, thrown upward continuously, as if the road was a sieve separating the grain from the husks, as if there was someone below blowing air bubbles through a straw.

I heard a sound similar to that of a great beehive outside of their home, searching for a new place to settle. The sound grew louder and closer, the columns of dust spiraled and gathered into brown-gray, unclear shapes; fur balls from a cat I used to like to brush. I was afraid. The ground shook, the roar of the engines and the grinding of metal sheets on each other exploded loudly, and from behind the turn there came a gray truck, followed by another, and another. Personal carrier half-tracks followed, and fear, like a caterpillar cut in half, panicked.

It seemed as if the colors disappeared, that everything was sprinkled with ash. I looked at the material of my best dress— no longer special, in small forget-me-nots, but dirty, ordinary: the flowers wilted, the flower patches covered in ash. I cried and it might have been those tears which washed away the grayness from the world, because I had the courage to look into the faces of the men who sat on the trucks, in the cabs, on the half-tracks.

They all looked alike to me, as if they had all been birthed by the same huge, busy mother. They had beautiful carved faces of golden-pink skin, hair as light as the frame of an icon, and eyes the color of my dress. They had athletic figures. They looked wonderful, dangerous, and noble. They looked as if they had lost their way in this part of the world, as if they were here by accident, they had fallen out of the real story, turned into a mistake, into a rumor not yet whispered from mouth to ear.

These sunny faces stretched into a smudge of light, losing details. Before the dust settled, returning the colors, a motorcycle stopped in front of us: so huge that it had a third wheel on the side and something like a crib, polished black, like the shell of a beetle. A figure jumped off the motorcycle. I crossed myself three times and let my gaze fall, because I thought it might be the devil or one of his servants: covered in black leather, even his face shaded by strange glasses, I couldn't see the tail though because he was facing me.

He approached the *ławaczka*, stopped, I could see the tips

of his dusty shoes. He started to say something, but it sounded
ugly, I couldn't understand what he wanted, he spoke in some
hellish, spluttering way; his language was full of the sound
of snapping young birches and breaking rafters and nothing
linked with anything else, everything was disconnected from
everything else. I asked *Boh* to take away the unclean from me,
I asked and asked, squeezing my eyes shut until orange loaves
of bread whirled in front of my eyes. Only later did everything
go quiet, and I felt the touch of alien, naked skin. The smell
of starch. I thought it was my mother, returned to lift my face
toward the road. That the evil had gone, chased away by my
mother's skirts, with the black figure and motorcycle.

I allowed the alien, naked skin, which touched me under the
chin, to turn my face toward the sun. That's when my eyes fell
onto another's: the bluest, deepest, and most joyful ones, large
and gleaming, and incredibly sad. I thought that this must be
what the sea looks like, which I had heard of from the Jews in
Gródek. That's what I thought, water with no end, impossible
to cross, only drown in, and a moment later I started to sob,
because I understood that I was enchanted, imprisoned, and in
love, for better or for worse. I understood that *Haspadź* had just
used his seal—I smelled the wax of that seal. The Lord linked
our fates, his in black leather and mine in a flowery dress.

The man, pointing toward his own heart, said:

"Joachim."

He was looking at me.

"Joachim," he repeated. "*Und Sie?*"

I felt myself go red. His touch was still burning me under
my chin. The stains my tears left still burned.

"Sonia," I answered as quietly as possible, but he still heard
me.

"Sonia," he smiled. "*Sehr gut.*"

He went to the black crib next to the motorbike and took
out something from it. A sleeping, fluffy puppy: a small German

shepherd with ginger streaks. He gave me a beautiful leather collar.

"*Sonia und Joachim*," he said, then got on his bike and left, leaving behind clouds of dust.

I was left with the sleeping puppy. I didn't know what to do. I felt like a seed sown on stones. I turned the collar in my fingers, trying to read the strangely styled letters. I wasn't a fluent reader, only what the priest had taught me, and these weren't letters which I knew, because the Cyrillic letters in our church look like chairs, but I managed to read this.

"Borbus," I said, and that's when the puppy lifted its head toward me.

That's how it got its name. Borbus the First.

"Borbus," Igor repeated.

"Borbus," Sonia repeated after him and got up to pour some more milk.

And on the other side of the window, Borbus, Borbus the Twelfth, whined quietly in the sunlight. Igor mentally put aside his pen, sheet of paper, smartphone, Dictaphone, and the electronic bank statement where Sonia's story was being written. He wondered whether the earlier Sonia should be more accented than this one—that depended on whether one looked from the current position, or from Warsaw—jargons, whether certain phrases, metaphors, similes should be eliminated, urban ones that Sonia would never think of. Or perhaps she would?

I have to emphasize the universal character of the story, he thought, this story which I can sense, but which I haven't yet heard. This story must, first and foremost, be understandable to others, because then it will also be understandable to me.

He swallowed a sip of milk.

"So your name is Sonia," he said. "I'm Igor. Igorek."

Sonia thought that there's no such name, not here. Maybe *Ihar*? There was no "g" in Sonia's language. It didn't matter— baring dentures and pointing toward her chest with her hand, she said:

"Sonia. Sońka."

We've discovered each other's names, he thought, leaving some room for lies.

And then unpleasant thoughts plagued him.

Sonia was silent. She felt happiness and contentment spreading over her forgotten and disregarded body. Once again in August something important would happen, once again it would be something final. She got up and took out a rag from her chest in the bedroom, which she handed over to her guest with some embarrassment.

"*Na, pahladzi,*" she said loudly.

The guest took his time unwrapping the rag. He weighed it in his hands at first, somewhat surprised, somewhat curious. It didn't weight much, but that which is important doesn't, just like that which is unimportant—that's why it's so easy to mix the two up, to make a mistake and get lost.

Igor looked at the burnt material. He was holding a bouquet of flowers, and a dirty, ripped rag with a huge brown stain. He focused his eyes on that stain: coffee, cocoa?

"*Heta jaho krou,*" Sonia said quietly.

I gave the puppy milk with some soaked bread. I was afraid father wouldn't let me keep the present. He came back very drunk, so drunk he didn't even have a go at hitting, he just fell onto the straw mattress and fell into a deep sleep, and I wished that sleep was a millstone around his neck, that the millstone would pull him into the depths so father would feel the night and cold, bats in his hair and leeches on his eyelids, that he would be afraid and swim out changed—better for Janek and Witek, better for me and *żywina*.

Because father is the devil. The devils have hatched in him, they're so hardworking and reverential. Father was no different than other fathers—here in all the villages the devils are so thickly sown that a camel couldn't squeeze through to paradise.

I couldn't sleep. Everything in me had changed. That's why I walked out in front of the house, to the bench where I sat a few hours earlier: once upon a time. I broke father's rule. "*Pa noczy tolki katy i bladzi łaziać*," he said. I was afraid of my willfulness, and even more of my own courage. Everything in me had changed. I was just the same and completely unlike myself, turned inside out like a dress. I was more afraid of the future than father's wrath, because the wrath I was familiar with, but the future—no. I gazed at the sky. I gazed at the dome with a million stars. *Mój Haspodź*, I prayed, you have a million stars, give me one, the smallest, knock one off with a finger or a sneeze, and I'll make a wish. One of the tiniest stars, it can be one of the bruised ones, I beg of you, give it to me.

And clearly my mother must have spoken for me to *Świataho*, because He picked a star, maybe it wasn't big, but solidly made and almost new, and He let it down to earth. I squeezed my eyes shut and made a wish. I kept my eyes squeezed shut for a long time, and my wish burned a fiery seal on my heart. It was a wish like the lid of a coffin. It was a brief wish, at most one word, probably less.

"Joachim," Igor said, echoing Sonia's greedy, unhappy wish in a calm voice.

Sonia looked at the city youth with wide eyes, the golden and balding one, with a receding hairline that resembled a slow river, the boy with an expensive scent and with no sweat stains under his arms, who was getting older, becoming clearly and almost wiser with every minute. The boy who came from the invisible place far away, to listen, understand, and bid Sonia farewell. The boy who had in him something that made one want to take him home, though it wasn't clear for how long.

Sonia looked at him and she couldn't stop, her nostrils pulled in the smell of starch from a million years ago, her eyes saw that star from before the Deluge, solidly made and definitely not bruised, as in the end the wish—at most one word, probably less—had come true immediately.

And from her right eye, from which color had been faded by the years, a large tear fell. It wasn't lively; first it formed slowly, slowly, to detach with difficulty. It wasn't a clear tear, but a milky white one. It wasn't a wet tear, only mildly damp. The tear was really a grain of salt. And it marched over the wrinkles on Sonia's face as a caterpillar might over an old twisted leaf, with no hope for transformation or metamorphoses, until at last, giving the lips a wide berth, it fell from the chin onto the floor, where it shattered into salty grounds.

And when the tear left its trace, Sonia's right eye regained its color. It was blue: a deep and joyful blue, gleaming and sad.

"You have Joachim's eye," Igor whispered.

"*A ty majesz krou na rukach,*" she replied.

Igor glanced at the bundle in his hands. There was no dirty rag with a large brown stain anymore. He was looking at a thin canvas. From the ceiling (so thought Igor) fell drops, the roof was leaking, filling the dried stain of blood with fresh blood;

history takes a new tribute; history is like a leech. Igor realized only after a moment that the fresh blood came not from the ceiling, but from his own nose.

"I'm sorry, I should lie down for a moment. Sorry."

With his head tilted back he kneeled, then stretched out on the kitchen rug. On his back. Sonia brought him a pillow. She made a compress from a white cloth after soaking it in cold water.

"*Laży, ja razkażu.*"

The bleeding ceased, Igor fell silent, an indescribable story writing itself in his head, black letters and lights of Jupiter, comments for the scenographer and anger at the lighting technician, and he only lay on the multicolored rug; the spider on the ceiling observed the slim figure cut out of the rainbow *szmatnik* with six eyes. Sonia licked her fingers. The chocolate turned out to be salty, exotic like the sea and melting on skin; delicious.

Sonia opened the window. The cat jumped onto the table, it was as old as Sonia, composed of scars and clumps of fur, of memories of lost battles and dreams of victory, of an allegory of a tail and an identity devoid of ideals such as nation or species, but full of mammal optimism that cats don't differ from each other more than by their coloring. It was the ugliest cat not only in all of Królowe Stojło, but in all of Europe. It was also one of six hundred and sixty-six cats in the world currently approaching the end of its ninth life. And a cat who approaches the end of its ninth life is not just a cat, the murderer of rats and a speaker to share its purring that is so pleasurable for the human joints. In his fifth life, Jozik worked to deserve the title of Mouse Shepherd, and such cats were rarer than Roman popes.

Jozik the cat arched his crippled back like a broken horseshoe. Sonia put her hand on him and closed her eyes. Jozik purred sparingly. He didn't care for caresses; he'd drifted a long way from sex, even of the stroking kind. He knew that his mistress, Sonia the Limper, loves her cat Jozik. That's why he stuck to his decision from his first life, when he decided to look after his mistress. He jumped to the ground. He carelessly walked over Igor's body, which had the unsettling sense of being someone else's, and curled up on the *leżajka*. He had a good view of the kitchen from here and—through the window—of the yard. He looked at Sonia, looked, and then fell asleep, because he was no longer a cat interested in the world: he had nine lives under his belt and some striped fur—that's enough to persuade any thinking animal to sleep.

I was afraid to open my eyes. Something was rubbing against my legs. It purred. It was the cat, Wasyl, similar to Jozik as any cat resembles another, but it had one white spot on its belly, and Jozik has nine. Wasyl went to the forest in spring, always, for the last three years, and it would return, overfed, before winter. Father threatened that he would drown Wasyl, but Wasyl was too cautious or father too drunk—it ended with threats, a few thrown stones, and meowed indignance.

I was afraid to open my eyes. The star had probably finished its fall. I didn't know what it brought other than the cat. I felt a warm breath on my cheek. It smelled of strawberries with cream and sugar. And how strongly! Suddenly I was ravenous. Ravenous for food and blood! I was dying of hunger! I was as hungry as a bear, my stomach was rolling on the other side of my belly button and the world. Hunger gnawed at me from the inside.

Sonia laughed at the memory of this hunger, which over-whelmed her on a certain August night in '41 (once upon a time, moments before the Deluge) and renewed itself, some-times more than once a day, for years.

Sonia had a silvery laugh, she laughed like a wise and noble Vestal, keeping alight the black fire like an incorruptible guardian of a secret, like a child on a romp. Because Sonia knew that this smell let loose another hunger: a hunger the existence of which she had not suspected, a hunger she had witnessed in her brothers, in Janek and Witek, and in father. Father's hunger ate her though, while hers, so similar, sated her instead.

Sonia laughed a young and contagious laugh, as if youth itself was contagious, as if Sonia had caught youth from Igor, who, stretched out on the kitchen floor, caught laughter off of Sonia and was growing thinner, ever more transparent. He was growing transparent to reveal someone else.

They laughed like this in unison, making Borbus the Twelfth wag her tail, and Jozik the Mouse Shepherd lifted an eyelid, with a few last eyelashes on it, to see whether his ninth and final life had ended.

Strawberries, sweet cream, and sugar—that's what the air on my cheek smelled of, straight from the plate, a promise of dessert. I opened my eyes. He stood before me in a black uniform, but it was night, color didn't matter. I was the one who walked toward him and took his hand. I felt an electric shock. I quietly voiced my wish, breathing in: Joachim. I was overjoyed: happiness filled me like air does a frog, it overfilled me and ran toward the fields and meadows under the eiderdowns. Ants marched over me, but only underneath, under me, under the skin hidden in blood.

I brushed silver dust off his shoulders. My fingers traced his pale face. That's when he embraced me. A bolt of lightning exploded in my brain. We fell to the ground as if we had been struck by a cannonball or a bullet. It didn't even cross my mind that we should hide. It was, after all, the night of my wish. Nothing threatened us. We lay next to the bench, kissing, grabbing naked skin from under clothes. I knew nobody would see us even if they stopped at arm's length. The night of my wish hid us like a mother's skirts.

I tried not to call out, I cried, our skin sparked. We were stuck as close as magnets, like mating dogs.

And so it was that we sealed our own fate. The fresh seal of the Lord cooled when we lay next to each other. It smelled of wax and incense, of ash and burnt flesh. Of fluids that I had no names for. I think that even then—once upon a time—we understood: this beginning, this night of a wish come true, the power of joined bodies, that was our end, the beginning of the fall.

I prayed passionately for the fall to last a long time, years and decades, for the Germans to win and stay with us forever, but this time the wise *Boh* cried no star as He looked down on our happiness.

Our downfall ripened in us, but we were prepared to pay any

price for the other person and our shared time; even a price higher than the highest—it wouldn't have been expensive. Even dishonesty, betrayal, and a loss of morality. Even a lied confession and torn dress. Even that.

Sonia sighed. She had said more than she thought, and she thought more than she felt. In reality all these judgments of her own fate didn't mean much to her: words were words, and the dead remain dead.

We lay in an embrace. Nothing broke the silence. I heard only father's snoring through the wall. It was the happiest night of my life. We didn't speak, why would we, we would have to talk in different languages. We barely ever spoke, Joachim and I.

It's untrue that time flies for those in love. Time flows differently, but it doesn't speed up. The eyes gaze heavily and carefully. Eyelids droop. Every shared minute seems longer, bigger, and deeper than a year spent alone. Oh yes, I remember every minute we shared, I could talk for hours about what I felt, what happened, what smelled, what hooted, which dog in which yard barked and where exactly the grass blades tickled my body. Every shared minute was a little eternity, a perfect world, every minute spent apart was as if thrown in the mud, broken and of little value.

I loved till the end, up to the boundary beyond which there is nothing. We loved each other so much that time flowed only when we were together. As if we were time itself. There was no time outside of us, none at all.

Joachim left. I didn't sleep a wink. I got up before the first crow of the rooster. I let the chickens out, shared out grain, collected the eggs, milked Malina and Zorka, the cows Janek later took to graze on the fields and into the woods. I started the fire *u pieczy*, I brought in water. I steamed potatoes for the pigs. I gave milk to Borbus and Wasyl. I prepared the *taukanica*, it's steamed and roasted potatoes on the *plicie* with pork rind, if we had those . . .

Father and Wasyl went to pick mushrooms. I did what I did every morning, though for the first time I felt no fatigue. The world around me had become translucent and half-transparent, made of fluff, from the sounds of geese, of ducks, and can such a translucent, fluff-filled bucket weigh as much as a real one?

I thought about Joachim, about the nearest night we would

spend together. Because only by being together did we make
color return to the world and the weight, fabric and smell,
truth and goals, heaven and hell. Without Joachim the world
resembled your modern foil bags: poorly made, disposable, and
sticky—so there is no way to get rid of it.

The day, filled with a variety of activities, ended quickly,
I didn't even have the chance to properly recall everything
Joachim and I experienced the previous night. I barely reached
the moment when the bolt of lightning exploded in my head,
when I was struck by a cannonball or bullet. Father and my
brothers, tired from work, didn't notice any change in me, I
don't think. Kicking the tiny Borbus so that the puppy flew two
meters, whining, father only asked: "*Skol heta barachło?*" I told
him about the Germans and he spat on the ground. He said
nothing. Not a word.

I didn't know what father thought: was he afraid of the
present? Was he satisfied with the new dog? I don't know. Niutka
from a neighboring house once spoke of my eldest sister Toma.
I never knew her; she—at three years old—got sick. Mother
wanted to send her to the folk healer, but father just spat. Toma
died that night. I thought that with that spit father had given
his verdict on the case of Borbus, just as he had on my sister's
life. And I decided that, against all odds, even if I had to leave
my home and go, tainted, elsewhere, I wouldn't let anything
happen to that dog.

I don't know who, the good *Boh* or my mother, who
churned everything like one would butter, who oiled the gears
of nightly darkness so I might sneak out and in without getting
caught, like an eel slipping from the hand into water. Joachim
and I met after dusk, usually close to the wooden bridge that
led to Słuczanka, and then we walked: to the fields, the forest,
the river, into the barn and the hay. Joachim was stationed in
Waliły, then after a month he was moved to Gródek, and he
conquered the kilometers between us easily, on horseback. The

gray gelding was called Pegasus. It was probably a German name, a commandeered name, but nevertheless pretty, full of feathers and movement. I liked it, I liked everything then: from mucking out with *wiła*, through feeding the pigs, to the evenings at the Orthodox church; and this required walking for many kilometers, or taking the wagon.

For two weeks, I barely ate or slept. I worked during the day, and at night I saw Joachim. The *krapiwa* in the swamps never smelled the same after this, nor were the squeaks of bats or the blinding moth wings the same. The world, even though it was seen at night, was sharp and clear. Wasyl sometimes walked me as far as the bridge. I heard how carefully he placed his paws. He waited for Joachim with me, looking with green eyes for somewhere to disappear into.

After two weeks of such working and not eating, after two weeks it became clear to my father, to Janek and Witek, to the neighbors, that something was going on with me. I was beginning to resemble the world around me, that is, the world that was Joachim, the world which was turned inside out like a caftan; semi-transparent, translucent, consisting of poplar fluff with seams on the outside. I couldn't even use my legs to knead the cabbage, because without weight, one can trample the veined leaves for a long time, without faith, one can recite the *Wieruju wo jedinoho Boha Otca* fruitlessly and for a long time, without existing, it's difficult to be. I gained flesh and kilograms only at night, only Joachim's touch brought back the blood to my veins, only then did the grass bend beneath me.

"*Skaży, jak można polubi tak druhoho cząławieka? Czamu? Pa szto?*" Sonia asked.

Igor lay on the colorful *szmatnik*. He didn't answer, because Sonia wasn't expecting an answer. It wasn't a question, but clearly expressed surprise and respect for what she had experienced with Joachim once upon a time, long, long ago. It was meant for anyone who has lived through something similar, something that crossed the boundaries of understanding, even feeling. Something omnipotent. Something else. As if metaphysics was a word that only sometimes made contact with the world.

Igor lay. With every day that passed in Sonia's story he felt older, thinner, like papyrus, and flaking like oil paint, as if some blue accountant was adding those days to his own life's bill, taking them away from Sonia's bill. Because of this she was looking younger, while he lost strength and the will to—since the bleeding had stopped—get up and maybe eat something or start fussing over his insurance. At the end of the day the car would fix itself.

People are easily found in rural areas, whether they want to be or not, unless they die, then it's like a stone in water, nobody said anything, heard anything, felt anything, just an ordinary splash. A village is a small world, within hearing and seeing distance, everyone lives so close to each other that nobody can miss anything, and then—punishment, rarely just. I slipped out of our *chata* as usual. Father and my brothers slept a heavy, flat sleep, as if after consuming poppies. Wasyl rubbed against my legs past the fence. He meowed, high and pitiful. I leaned down to stroke him. That's when I thought I heard something, something like splintering twigs, a held breath, and a bead of sweat forming between breasts. I made my way to the bridge. I spotted Joachim immediately: in my eyes, for which daylight was increasingly bright and blinding, a clear outline was reflected, a dark envelope. The two steel lightning bolts on his uniform glimmered. I thought that those lightning bolts, so close to one another, brightened in a blinding flash—were us.

I kissed him and took his hand. For the first time he was tense all over, hard and distant. He was all angles, without circles or diagonals. We walked down to the river, and he began to tell some story. At first I thought it was this kind of story.

Soon, the war will be over. There will be no front, I won't be needed here. I'll take you to my mother, she has a beautiful villa close to the German town of Haradok. Father died two years ago, he was a teacher. Mother will be happy. I'm sure she'll love you. Mother tells the past and future; she's bipolar. Then we'll get married. You'll cook *polnische* food, sometimes. Everyone will like it. We'll have five children: Waschil, Griken, Jan, Phrosch, Schiessen. We'll go to resorts and to the seaside (in German the sea is *Juden*). We'll have a cat called Raus. The cat will lie in the sun and catch *Schweine* (which is mice in German). The neighbor, an elderly man wearing a striped suit, *Herr* Abramowitsch, will write us into his will. And another neighbor, also from *Polen*, Mr. Buchwald, will marry his daughter to our firstborn.

I really thought at first that it was such a story. The panic fluttering in me when I saw Joachim muddled my mind so much that I didn't know what I knew. People talked. The panic pounded against my insides like dry peas against the walls of a can. With every sentence I realized that I understood too much in this lack of understanding; the names of our unborn children sounded suspiciously familiar, distorted only in the hoarse dialect. Then I heard a different story, tearing its way up through the first one; I had heard this different story hundreds of times already, not from Joachim's lips, but from those who had lived or seen, or who fought to drive off the nightmare as if it were flames, waving their arms and stoking it instead. But maybe the story wasn't about them at all, but about my brothers and husband? Or maybe it wasn't at all yet, but will be?

They gathered over one hundred people close to the wooden synagogue in Gródek, the one which stood close to the Orthodox church. It was a hot day. The Jews stood in a tight group. They were afraid. There were shopkeepers, barmen, tailors. Their families. Those who still owned something: maybe not much, but nevertheless, they had something. They had bookkeeping notes in notepads, nightmares about Yahweh, because their God was worse even than ours, they had bar mitzvahs on their minds and girls to marry off. They spread their arms helplessly, stuffed their hands into pockets, squeezed their palms into fists.

They were older men, smelling of dust and oil from lamps; there were also younger men, smelling of sunshine and fresh sweat. Behind the cordon of soldiers, the inhabitants of Gródek gathered. Some of them pitied, some didn't understand, some hoped to pay off their debts. Some were even amused by the humiliation of their poorer neighbors, some were horrified.

The soldiers first pulled out a young boy from the tightly knit group. "*Sehr gut*," Joachim said; just as he'd once said to me. The soldier pulled out the Mauser from its holster, placed the barrel against the temple and pulled. Nothing else, a fountain of drops of blood and shattered bones.

Sonia was shaking her head as if she didn't understand much of what she was recalling, and what she hadn't seen with her own eyes. Maybe she had made it all up? Maybe in the collision of story and history, it is truth that always emerges, battered? Igor lay tense. Individual pains, for instance his own, even if it wasn't too far from tonsillitis, were not borne easily by him, and massive pain, planned up above and carried out down here— paralyzed him. He couldn't listen, he was sympathetic automatically, in an unconditional reflex of blunt solidarity.

In the bright spark which jumped to him from Jozik the Mouse Shepherd, he understood that he must remember even more than Sonia was telling him, he has to harness his mind to a theatrical or prose treadmill to save himself, to finally tell a truth, fight for something. Though he had suspected as much from the start, from the threshold.

The boy fell. *Baciuszka* would repeat that *Boh* raises the fallen and strikes down those still standing. *Boh* didn't raise the boy, didn't push in the drops of blood and fragments of bone. Was the Jewish Yahweh not as forgiving or omnipotent? After all, at ours in Haradek He was like in a foreign land—far away from the deserts, a vagrant. Or perhaps we weren't deserving? After all it didn't matter to the boy anymore, the unhappiness was born in others, it was others who needed a miracle and reassurance. It seemed we didn't deserve Lazarus. Though Lazarus, thinking about it, wasn't ours, and a Jew was like all the first *chryścijany*.

Apparently nobody said anything. The Germans dragged people out one by one, placed barrels against heads, and pulled triggers. Every such fall pulled a few people from the circle of observing neighbors. These people went home, but not to their own. Witnessing the shopkeeper's death, they made their way to the abandoned shop. Witnessing the tailor's death, they went to the ownerless establishment.

In the end there was only old Mr. Buchwald and *baciuszka* and the Catholic priest. That's when the Germans walked away, suddenly, leaving almost a hundred corpses behind them, three survivors, and clouds of flies. The Germans just walked away, as if this event didn't matter, as if time for work had ended and it was time for rest. Almost a hundred corpses, three survivors, and clouds of flies.

That was, maybe, Joachim's story. I no longer thought that *Juden* meant sea in German, that *Raus* was a cat, that *Schweine* meant mice. I had the most pity for Joachim. I loved him and he was still alive, but I still pitied him, I couldn't do otherwise. My poor, bright Joachim, his beautiful body, now traced with the twisted silhouettes of corpses.

Joachim stopped speaking. To this day I don't know what

he was trying to tell me that night: about the future and the murder in the town, or about the future after the murder or about the future without a future, I don't know. He squeezed my hand tightly. It hurt, but the pain was nothing compared to what he was feeling. He started to cry. He talked and cried, with no relationship between the two. Then he laid his head on my breast and fell silent. I breathed with a bag of stones on my chest.

We didn't sit there for long. He didn't even kiss me goodbye, just touched my shoulder, my breast; my nipple hardened.

I watched him as he walked away: he had vanished into the dark a long time ago, but I still stood motionless, wondering if my Joachim was a nocturnal vision or a man of flesh and blood.

/Now we will show documents about the murder of Jews in Gródek.

There is a film with recovered photographs, no longer than three or four minutes.

In paper form there are about ten photographs, including NEC-ESSARILY at least one with a child./

Someone touched my shoulder.

"*Ty ni swaja. Ty bladź.*"

I didn't know who spoke those words. I was still reeling from the fact that Joachim didn't kiss me goodbye, or that he didn't come into me for hello. The words hurt me, but also made me happy, because it was proof that Joachim was real. Then the foreign voice pushed me over, I fell, and he choked me to the ground. I was on my stomach, with sand in my nose and between my teeth. My tongue had attached itself to the ground so surely I couldn't pull it in. A hand was suffocating me with huge force. Then the other hand of the foreign voice pulled up my dress.

I tried to protest, but it was all for nothing. I was like a child protesting against the unjust decision of her parents. The voice was much stronger. I tried to throw him off of me, but after a few hits to the head I lost consciousness. A searing pain woke me. The voice was panting into my ear, droplets of sweat and spit fell on the back of my neck, his *struk* was tearing my body. He was raping me like a sheep, from behind, trying to cause the most pain. I could barely breathe. Finally, he finished. He raised himself off of me. "*Ciaper srać ni budziasz, job twaju mać.*" I couldn't move. Warm fluid filled my ear, flowing to my mouth. It was his urine. Blood, feces, sperm, urine.

(Local patriotism, thought Igor.)

I lay like that for a long time, I think. Only a dog's tongue returned some life to me. I don't know how Borbus made his way out of the yard. Father tied him up because he strangled neighboring chickens. Then, some people helped me stand and took me home: a man and a woman, or maybe I was alone? Maybe I only made them up because that's how much I didn't want to be alone in my degradation?

And was that war real? Or only in my head?

It was getting darker outside, Borbus the Twelfth barked, Sonia got up and lit the light with an archaic, twisting light switch. The light bulb with a tungsten thread bored into Igor's head, creaking like a dentist's drill, which is why he got up off the floor. How quickly the hours passed, he thought, how much I'm used up.

(And I hope that the cows didn't scratch the car with their horns, he added, I don't know if the insurance covers cattle.)

Indeed, in the unfocused light Igor could see liver spots on his hands, the dry skin on his forearm, he could see individual gray hairs on his calves, blades of frost, he could see the other in himself, from the past, from the beginning; he might have to paw after all.

He wasn't scared that he had caught the illness of age, he only thought that the contrast of a fairy tale with myth ruined the body. And that childhood stays in a person forever, like seasons and cruelty: it could be denied, but never killed, painted over, or forgotten—at best one can erect a screen.

Sonia's body, in contrast, looked firmer, even her breasts stretched the fabric of her dress, even her hair escaped from under the flowery headscarf in glimmers of gold—not mercury or silver—wheat shines like that, in and of itself, straight into the eye.

Sonia walked outside to the front of the house, and her guest followed. Night fell unexpectedly. The glow of the stars rubbed gothic letters on the collar of her dress, they shone now, cold and blue. Sonia took Igor's arm: in that moment, she seemed to be the younger of the two. The makeup artists had really done an outstanding job.

They went toward the river. Green cat eyes glowed beyond the fence.

"This is where the bridge was," she said. "Now it's different. Cement. And without Joachim. And without war. Ah," she almost shouted, "how I miss the war! Why did it end?!"

Igor completed the walk many times later, referring to it as documentation. Mostly at night, because during the day he interviewed the inhabitants of Królowe Stojło and the proud microcosmic Słuczanka. He asked about Sonia. What was she like? Speak freely, for she's no longer among the living.

The people said: "white" or "lame." Or: "good." And this meant nothing, like air in the lungs, like a dodge, apnea.

Why did they let her live until her natural death? Not from pity or kindness. The situation seemed hopeless, nobody wanted to talk to Igor; the answers sealed shut, under lock and key, the heart soundless in the breast, hay, they excused themselves with hay. Until Igor reached more surely into his younger years, in which he held his earliest memories of interhuman communications in the east. He recalled that here, on the borders of civilization, a serious conversation began after two bottles of moonshine.

He drank a lot with the locals. He even began to like some of them, in a strange way. They didn't read, they never went to the theater or cinema, and to the house of culture—called only the dayroom, because for a long time there were only candles there, no electricity—only when they gave something away or gave orders. They fed themselves with television and the Orthodox church, a few with the Church, and everyone—with rumors. Rumors gave meaning to the empty hours, devouring them, so that before they knew it they had lived their lives. It was like pepper. And salt. Like taste. Like a stem's core. Like rhubarb. Blood of blood, anger of anger, envy curdling the milk.

Igor befuddled their fortitude. They didn't forget or forgive. And he would have hated them and looked down on them in his middle-, almost upper-class, way, if it wasn't for the fact that they also avoided carrying out punishment. They could also suffer for a long time, with no complaints. They didn't expect justice, they weren't mad, they adapted to the history that ate into the world like a worm into a body. A strange species of man, Igor thought. It deserves a deep respect, it doesn't raise pity, sometimes it disgusts. It's difficult to think anything explicit about the locals. And I have to remember that I'm from here, too.

After a while, after liters of alcohol, they began to talk.

Sońka was a folk healer.

She could cast a spell on a cow to make it die. On the sow, so it only had stillbirths. On the bride, so she would be spotted with acne before the wedding, so that her nipples swelled to the size of a saffron milk cap.

Sońka was, others said, our punishment for the horrors of the war. Our memory, said those most drunk and reminiscent, we are bad, bad, and she was the worst of us all. The worst, because she doesn't regret. She doesn't regret, the bitch, doesn't give a fuck or a drop of blood, not even the tiniest bit of dirt under a nail.

Sońka, she helped, others said, she knew how to use ash for spells. She chased away illness, cured animals. She knew cupping therapy.

Sońka wasn't too bad.

Only when working on the spectacle did Igor realize that men were the ones who usually spoke ill of her, and women—well. On the one hand, punishment, on the other, understanding, although even that is a lie.

They sat at the table after the evening walk. Jozik the Mouse Shepherd was warming his paws, Borbus was curled into a ball under the table. They sat over the glazed enamel cups with decaf coffee. There was steam rising from them, and from everything else, from the wet fields and the river. Remnants, Igor thought, remnants of her and myself, and the remnants of animals that ended the lineage: the twelfth dog and ninth cat.

"*Lapiej pamirać u łóżku, u swajoj chaci. U szpitalu feko.*"

In a way he agreed with that, he'd prefer to die in his own home rather than a hospital, nevertheless he stood up and nervously paced the kitchen: the door to the hallway, four steps, door to the room, four steps, turn around, four steps. Death made him nervous.

"*Ni pamrecie*," he said, even though he didn't really believe it. It was Ignacy who said this, pawed free of embarrassment, of denial, of shock.

It was the first time he spoke to Sonia not in Polish, but *pa prostu*—as they called this language. *Pa naszamu.* He wasn't sure himself whether it was Belarussian, or a Russian dialect, or perhaps Polish? A *trasianka*? An historical or emotional aberration? A people thrown out of textbooks? A nation without a history? That's how his grandparents used to speak, his parents and he himself, until he forgot in order to live his life without basic linguistic humiliation.

Ah, the first language, milk from socialization, pride for no reason, embarrassment without fault. His parents forgot the language first, when they moved to the medium-sized city of Białystok. They had to work, and they could only work in Polish, they did, after all, live in Poland, that's why they remembered to *pa prostu*—forget. If they forgot to forget, they would immediately be branded Russkis: it would mean the end of friends, of work, of a newer and better life in a newer and better fatherland. And social advancement, who could help themselves after such poverty and hurt? His national ID card was sufficiently tried by the category "place of birth"; having Słuczanka fill it out raised enough suspicion.

Ignacy learned quickly that if he wanted to have friends at school and around the house, he couldn't speak like his grandparents did. Speaking like that, he would have friends who were his grandparents' age, and those people didn't climb trees or shoot at cats from slings, they didn't pull girls' braids with ribbons tied at the ends. And school wasn't easy as it was. In the first lessons it was clear that Ignacy had received the worse lot. Ignacy—by being christened and confirmed all together, to welcome him into the world—got the smaller God.

Not the great and pure, Catholic and Polish, not the one who raised and lost uprising after uprising, bled until poetry was written, but the other, wrinkled, old Slavic Orthodox God, gibbering with the voices of village women and *mużyki* in sweet incense and darkened icons. His God, dwarf-like and rural, Orthodox and gilded—caused his friends and their mothers to look down on Ignacy from the heights of their starched, anti-communist faith, from St. Peter's throne which wasn't nearly as cool as that of John Paul II. And from such a height Ignacy was similar to his God, that is: damaged, collaborating with the Russians, unsure and worse.

When he left for the capital to study, he cut himself off from himself, took the name Igor, newer and prettier, and confirmed in his papers. And he elongated his surname. Instead of Gryki he was Grycowski, more worldly. And sometimes he regretted that, because of a sleeping pill, he didn't foresee that minorities would be in one day. He reassured himself though that they would go out of fashion: the world never favored the underdog.

As he walked—four steps, turn, four steps—it dawned on Igor that perhaps Sonia was right. That it was better not to rush to the doctor in matters of death, it was worth waiting until the morning, until the sun rose. We're on the earth of my God, he thought, perhaps a small one, but I don't need anything great.

The opening night of *Królowe Stojło* was in the National Theater in Warsaw, out of season. On the anniversary of Sonia's death. Everyone attended. Some because they wanted to see for themselves that Igor Grycowski was finished, and the three-hour-long play would be the three-hour-long process of the last nail going in the coffin, though without excessive enthusiasm and frequent invitations from morning television, directors, and literary personae. Others, because they were curious what he had spent so much time working on in secret. Others still, because they always appeared where they should. Besides, there were refreshments and drinks served as compensation, always a good remedy for a moving artistic experience.

As *Viva!*—the colorful magazine of rumors aimed at women who could more or less fit letters together, and turn the pages in order—diligently related, only one critic left during the production, apparently the greatest national memoir writer, who made his name by crumpling references to the Holocaust into modern culture, especially advertisements.

Królowe Stojło was icily received by critics, with no atmospheric warming. It was difficult to believe, when reading the reviews, that so many mistakes could have been made in a three-hour-long production—that in itself deserved a prize or at least a medical insurance payout. Feminists attacked the gross neo-conservitism, so terrible probably because it didn't acknowledge second-wave feminism. (OMG, Igor said, reading a review about what his production didn't include; *Królowe Stojło* didn't include many things, for instance landing on the Moon. And WTF does "intersectional analysis" mean?!—which he had been unexpectedly praised for.) Conservatives, also those preceded by a neon neo-, couldn't agree with the history's vision: history isn't a hump, a fungal infection, or a motherfucker taught to people by people, but a value which was trampled upon and denigrated, a value above values, hallelujah, Battle of Warsaw and the laser rays of the Holy Mother, defeating the Bolsheviks in case of a future need to raise financial aid from the faithful. The Belarussians were unsatisfied—which wasn't strange in and of itself, as they were always unsatisfied, that's what happens to nations which are suffocated for centuries— because they felt that locality is less than the nation, and there were footnotes to Belarussian speeches everywhere, in the theater program and book, as if Belarussian wasn't "simply" understood in Poland; so they were made into a minority and humiliated, but they still border Russia. For Poles from under the sign of the radiating planet Krypton and ultraviolet Burning Heart of Jesus it was overall a nightmare, not a word about the Warsaw Uprising and God's Mercy. Add to that too strange a staging, though at the same time also too classical, which made eyelids droop. Leftist critics asked if the liberal elites even knew how to be moved without Shoah nearby, although of course they acknowledge the Holocaust wholeheartedly, that is, in culture and references to it. And the LGBT minority was offended by the heteronormativity—atrocity! backwater! in a heteronormative edition! In summary: nobody was satisfied: a bother and waste of time, lollygagging at the Vistula with a stick, and a kayak at the Oder, the critics claimed in polyphonic unity. The festival of turning one's nose up turned round and round like a prayer wheel or a carousel. After reading ten crushing reviews Igor knew that he had been successful. It was an enormous success. For as long as he could remember, no production had been received so venomously. Turning pain and suffering into something moving was, after all, always a painful process. And frustrating. Nobody valued the production apart from the audience. And the audience banged on doors and windows, was moved enough to promise to change their own lives, sobbed and decided to be better. Nothing changes the urban man for the better like the chance to watch another's unhappiness. *Królowe Stojło* didn't disappear from the posters for subsequent seasons.

After a year, tastemaking journals and weeklies decided that since their negative opinion wasn't enough to dissuade the audiences, taste must be adapted to the readership. *Królowe Stojło* was promoted to the position of an immortal work: it was identified as Polish, Belarussian, German, and Jewish; also humanistic, let's not forget this word; and avant-garde and classical; moving, though not sentimental. Instead of tackiness people saw purposefully created tackiness, the air carried the smell of what Igor and Ignacy had already made their peace with, together, and laughed, because it was as if conscious shitting was culturally and politically different from simply excreting due to the intestines.

He watched the recording of the opening night on a large screen. He wanted for the ninth time the scene of the Walk under the Bridge.

Now he pauses and zooms in on the actress's face. He dims the background. Her face freezes, filling the screen. He stares into her half-closed eyes.

He spent the last week staring at her face. That face overwhelms and disarms him with honesty, or truth. He can see the work of the makeup artists, he can see the scene, all the imprecisions and imaginary creations, but he still believes that face.

He starts the recording again. The woman falls onto the fake grass. She breathes imperceptibly. The actor who plays Joachim sits next to her. They undress. Curtain. What's wrong with being after the original?

On a large stage in the middle of the room, with a scenography with flowery wallpaper and a ceiling of blue lights, stood a toilette with a mirror and plastic flowers. There was a set of polished furniture: a wardrobe, glass bookcase with crystal, a table and four chairs, fake flowers and holy pictures on thin paper. There was also a bed with a coverlet of multicolored patterns.

On their faces—the young face of the woman and Igor's ageing face—falls a delicate, golden glow. The angel at the headboard has spread its wings beautifully. Angel:

(Remember to speak to the lighting producer, Igor notes mentally, that angel looks like it's come from the Basement under the Rams.)

The decisions are not mine, mine are only the wings. That's why I spread them as fully and charmingly as possible, in magic and frills, in events and interpretations. My sweet, I saw you before you became an egg with the thread of a sperm, I saw everything, but still I didn't expect to see what I see. My lamest, most hobbling, dearest, I am your guardian, I am Gabryiel the Nineteenth, my place is at the head of a pin, right by the first: Michał and Samael. I am to protect you, lend a helping hand when you fall, I must-I must-I must, I-I-I will lift you!

Sońka lit the *piecza*. She prepared a milky soup with mash and salt. She boiled water for tea. It will be strong. Then she'll make a start on the cabbage and mushrooms, if she has enough time and strength. A special occasion at home: a guest, an angel, like Abraham's visit.

She tries to remember how this visit ended.

Possibly not well.

Sonia couldn't think of Joachim as a German. Germans shot, burned villages, commandeered food and animals. The Germans did her only one favor: they killed father.

When Sonia realized that father would never return in any other form than a nightmare, she cried from happiness. People counted, yes, but most of all cows and goats counted. Without them people starved. Just now, slurping the milky soup, she recalled that moment.

Father left before dawn to collect firewood. The whole village ran to the swamps to wait out the next march-through of German troops. Germans didn't really venture into unknown territory, unless they could find a guide. Between the trees, with loose, wet soil beneath their feet, the locals could feel relatively safe. There weren't many left. Every month of the war could be counted by the absences. In July, the Konstanciuk family had been shot, in August Władek Karpowicz was lost, in September someone found Gienia dead: with a bayonet wound running from her vagina up to her throat. Some died, leaving bodies behind, others vanished: they went to the fields or forest and never came back. Although all the deaths were attributed to the Germans, Sonia knew that neighbors lost their lives at the hands of neighbors, too. Spreading dislike, envy, hurt—everything swelled and grew in the body of the corpse and corpse. And corpse.

A dozen or so men harnessed horses to carts and headed to the forest. Winter was close; firewood had to be collected to survive. Winter was close, and the men, horses, and carts—were lost. No news. Were they lost to a German trap? Or had they been liquidated by guerrilla troops that warred among themselves?

No mass grave was ever found, no harness fragment, or a single horse. Nothing that could lead to any trail. Sonia thought that only Germans could organize such precise eradication. Yes, Sonia thought, the Germans were masters at arranging life through death.

And when Sonia realized that father wouldn't return—on the day in the swamps, waiting for another march-through of German troops, with a stomach as empty as a pocket with a hole—she cried from happiness; and then she cried when it dawned on her that she was happy because of a small part of the great reclamation, great correction, which was happening right in front of her, and simultaneously beyond her gaze, which trembled on eardrums in dry shots: somewhere there—somewhere nowhere, so long ago, before the Deluge, so that mold muffled the sound, and a bug rolled the body; it was a stitch of satisfaction in an indifferent world.

Disgraced and spat out, raised by Gabryiel the Nineteenth, licked by Borbus, with a calf opened by Wasyl. First, they walked down to the river, where Sonia washed the dirt off herself: blood, feces, and sperm, sweat and spit and earth, threads from her dress, hair, and tears. And history: the greatest atrocity that can touch a person and stick. To skin and thought. To the roof of the mouth like hot food. Then she made her way home. Then she lay down. The younger brother opened his eyes. "*Ty kurwa, mnie ustydna*," he said. He closed his eyes.

That night she couldn't sleep, and the night didn't want to end, as if someone had decided that that night Sonia would not sleep for all the sleepless nights. Sometimes she fell into apathy, which began with a pain in her anus. She walked the trail by the river with water up to her knees. The water was cold and brown. Every once in a while she threw a primitive fishing line, to catch a large fish. The fish, resembling pike with sharp teeth, or stinking catfish, fought among themselves, and she was afraid and surprised all at once, that they didn't hurt her, and she threw the line again and again. She pulled out a fish again and again, and they fought each other in the brown water. They didn't bite her: she had already been hurt, after all.

The brown water and slipperiness of the fish skins turned out to be nothing next to father's and her brothers' brutality after she woke. They didn't say anything, they pushed her more often than usual. Sonia was under the impression that they knew everything about her and Joachim. Almost everything, because if they knew everything they would not be so cruel and thoughtless.

The buckets were no longer translucent, the potatoes weighed more, like on some usurious scales, the pigs' appetites seemed to outweigh the trough, Gargantua and Pantagruel. The chickens only annoyed her with their clucking. Only Borbus, Borbus the First and the Aryan, helped her in her daily chores with his carpet of fur rubbing against her legs. When the chubby pan of the sun lit up the grass with a fire that rose to the sky, Sonia realized two things: first, that she had survived the worst day of her life, and second, that the worst day of her life was leading toward nothing.

Joachim didn't wait for her. After this day, the night awaited Sonia. An ordinary night, perhaps a calm one, one with sleep. Without rape. But without Joachim, too. If rape was the price she had to pay to meet her lover, she would do so many times. She was rich. She paid her father before Joachim appeared. Despite the disgust she felt toward herself, the dirt she couldn't wash off, she could pretend to be pure for Joachim. She could change, stop being Polish, Russian, or one of us. She could stop being anything. She could still herself in the air like a dragonfly—a clap of the hands is enough to squash me.

It would be enough if Joachim wanted to look at her. For him to make his way to the bridge that led to Słuczanka. Sonia saw the bucket lips curve into the shape of Joachim's lips. Sonia heard the rooster crow eerily. Sonia saw the trough into which she threw the slops for pigs arch its wooden vertebrae, so similar to the body which bent her own body into violins and flourishes. Sonia saw different eyelashes in the water, light, as if burning; she saw eyes into which she would throw herself before the fire touched the lashes.

Sonia saw different things, she saw them everywhere, she saw them day after day, but Joachim didn't return. She slept, she rose, she ate and stroked Borbus's soft fur as he grew taller than her knees and almost never barked.

Sonia loved, because it was so easy to die. Sonia ate, because it was so easy to starve. Sonia felt, because it was so easy to stop feeling altogether.

Sonia was becoming the neighborhood madwoman. The position of village idiot had been vacant for ten years, since old Irka died. Sonia didn't know that in Spanish (which she didn't know, just as she didn't know that there was such a country somewhere far away), *ira* meant "anger" and "rage," as if anger and rage, as if fury was attached to every slender and abandoned person, every person who was abandoned and not at all dangerous—hurt and abandoned. Because the insane were physically eliminated by the village. A group of peasants gathered, pitchforks, axes, a few blows, and mass. Such a peasant was decent, such an accident was a shame, bad luck. That was all that was. Not much. And it was always the fault of the Germans. Or the Russians. Or nobody's, when it was a time of peace, so God's punishment.

The night was deep. Jozik the Mouse Shepherd wondered whether he should go to the barn and watch the mice, he could eat something living and velvet, something crunchy and squeaky, but the warmth that beat from the *leżajka* convinced him to stay in the kitchen after all. He could sense impending death, though he didn't know whom it would claim: Sonia the White, Ignacy, Igor, or perhaps himself?

Ignacy returned to the kitchen, there was now much more of him than of the Warsaw Igor. A single light bulb in green alabaster arranged shadows on the urban dweller's body as if tucking them in to sleep. His figure was composed of dark smudges. Muscles, somehow attached to bones, vanished in that strange light. Only the hairs, the gray ones, which he had worked for for thirty-odd years and the last day, only those glimmered: like in a market, like in a painting, something between glitter and varnish.

Ignacy sat down on the *słończyk* by the oven and watched Sonia. Sonia, with a face gently lit by the milky soup. Sonia with the white braid and the eyes that each seemed to glisten a different color.

I hadn't seen Joachim in two months. Apparently he had been sent to the eastern front. Autumn came from the east. After a plentiful summer autumn decorated itself with apples, pears, and bunches of rowanberries. I had never seen so much fruit. I had seen only a little.

Before the first leaves fell, it became clear—because it was visible—that I was pregnant. You can't know, *Ihnat*, what pregnancy means. A pregnancy in a village, without a husband. Without a wedding. Without a dowry. Father barely spoke to me. He didn't even give out orders. He didn't hit me or push me. As if he was disgusted by me. I became a cowpat: one had to step around it, not into it. It suited me because I had as much solitary time as one can have after doing all the farm chores: not much, a lot less than I would have been able to shoulder.

I was afraid of winter, in wintertime it congeals into the chatter of teeth. It congeals into ice and lips pressed together, into fists and elbows, blowholes must be cut to see the future months and some pale future. I was afraid of winter, I was more afraid for Joachim.

I dreamed that my bright Joachim sits in the gray shell of a tank. A closed hatch cut a few white feathers from his wings. Burning balls of fire fly from the cannon at regular intervals, hitting brown people with a bear's posture. A red star lights up in the hat of the monster at each blow. The monster falls, but two more appear in its place.

(A Lernaean Hydra, Igor thought.)

One evening, when half the leaves were already rotting under the tree crowns, father came back from the Gryks drunk and angry enough to push me to the ground straightaway. So furious that his eyes were a purple-red color with a spot of emptiness in the middle, a donkey penis shining in his face.

"*Trzymajcie dobra*," father said to my brothers.

Janek and Witek held me under my arms. I was never close with my brothers. We lived closely together because we had to. I wondered which one would inherit: the younger or the elder? They also wondered, and when a person wonders too much, they think too little and end up being obedient.

Janek seemed delicate, probably after mother, but his delicacy hid an incredible need to survive and dominate. I trusted him little because he spoke little. Witek wasn't similar. He grew big, with thick bones. He couldn't hide anything. One and the other were obedient, carrying out father's wishes.

Ihnat, I don't want to complain, but you need to know what in those days—once upon a time—being a woman really meant. Behind our hills and fields, behind our barns and troughs the value of a woman is no more than the value of a goat, though the goat had a better chance to survive, because it gave milk, and a woman only seldom and even then not for everyone.

Witek and Janek held me firmly, and father walked over and spat in my face. Then, his arm made a swing to hit me. Father could hit. The lip swelled, blood spurted like from a full glass. Nobody said anything. Father took the pitchfork and approached with it. He tore my jacket, exposing my body.

(The curtain was raised, Igor thought, the beginning of the second act.)

A white body, an emaciated one. With the beginnings of a belly. A body father knew well.

"*Heta czyj bastruk?*" he asked.

I tried to recall Joachim's image. So that he would protect me. Give me strength. Saint Joachim, from Sonia of Królowe Stojło, help me. Saint Joachim of the Conquered Land, save me. Joachim of the Bridge to Słuczanka, give me peace, Joachim, Fighter of Bears and shining red stars, hide me with a black coat, and punish my enemies with the lightning from your collar.

You don't know what it means to love without any sense, not the smallest bit of sense . . . I saw how Joachim's buttocks rose and fell in the moonlight. That image, the two half-globes of my lover's buttocks, like a moon cut in half, fuzzy with hair, covered father's swollen cheeks.

But father repeated his question:

"*Heta czyj bastruk?*"

I wanted to answer angrily: *twoj*, fear stopped me. Anger isn't as strong as fear. I was afraid for myself, and even more afraid—for our child. The answer surprised us all: father, my brothers, and myself.

"*Kareckaho*," I said.

I pointed toward the one I liked least. Misza Karecki, the third and youngest son of old Wańka, the poacher and kulak. Don't shine the lamp too strongly over his soul, Lord, but don't turn off the lamp, because it's inhuman to spend one's time freed from life in the darkness.

Misza, the youngest and the handsomest, the dearest son of the aged Wańka, didn't have the best reputation in Słuczanka, or in Królowe Stojło, or in the neighboring villages. They said he chased after skirts. They said that he was narrow-minded and cruel. They said many things, as always when not much was known, and time must somehow be spent together.

I rarely saw him, and had no desire to see more of him. I don't know why I chose him.

I could have told the truth, or I could have lied. I could have lied in a dozen different ways. I could have burdened so many men with my belly, both those less and more likely, though the belly—either way—was my own burden to carry. I chose him, because nobody would have believed it.

Sonia laughed, trying to chase away the memory of that moment, or maybe the opposite: that joke worked out for her like almost nothing else in her life.

"*Nathała ja*," she repeated.

"I also lied," Igor said.

That's when Jozik the Mouse Shepherd spoke. He was allowed to speak once in each of his nine lives, not counting, of course, Christmas Eve, though the cows were usually the first to the trough of words.

Cats don't lie, because they were formed from the most noble of materials: velvet fur, hard enamel, elastic, and pneuma. People, dogs, and mice lie. Especially mice. In reality, mice never speak the truth. They squeak. Mice are gray evil with a bare tail, evil which must have the breath knocked from it with a paw and be crushed. Chickens don't lie either, because they are made of feathers, a beak, and legs. In such a trinity there is no space for anything but grain.

Cats have wondered for centuries why people lie. A thousand years ago one of the greatest cats in the world, Osiris the Egyptian, meowed that it's the destructive influence of free will. But these cats also have free will, and I met only one cat, a she-cat actually, who spoke an untruth by assuming I had kittens. Such are cat issues.

"Achoo," Sonia said.

Father didn't beat me anymore, the hold of my brothers lessened. Father was calculating: Misza was the best bachelor in the area, it would be worth seeing how he reacted. If—almost certainly—he said "no," nothing would change. But if—which was unlikely— he said "yes," father would enter the elite of Słuczanka.

"*Idzi papratać, a ty,*" he shouted to Witek, "*paklicz na wieczar Wańku z Miszaj.*"

I went to clean, even though everything was clean. I cleaned anyway, and from all this cleaning the cleaned didn't get any newer or prettier, just older and more used, but time passed, albeit shabbily.

I heard how father was inviting Wańka and Misza over the threshold. They settled behind the table, I carried in hooch, salted bacon and marinated mushrooms, jars with preserves, sausages and cucumber. Stores for a rainy day or a religious holiday.

They drank and talked.

I was cutting an onion when father eventually said:

"*Znajesz, Wańka, maju doczku, Sońku?*"

"*Znaju. Jana udana wielni, wykapana Gala.*"

Hearing my mother's name, I cut my finger.

"*Jana ni feka, tolko sztom,*" father continued, "*ja tabie skażu sztoś wielmi śmiesznaho. Sońku, chadzi siudy, padydzi, doczeńka.*"

I walked over, sucking my finger.

"*Ty hladzi, jana panna, a z żywatom jak żonka.*"

Wańka, gray and dry, slid his gaze over me.

"*Żywot ni uziałsa z pawietra. Żywot Sońki uziałsa z Miszy.*"

Silence fell after father's words. Wańka understood why we were meeting. Misza's eyes jumped from face to face, like a flea jumps between dogs: with a reddened nose in a handsome face, with viscera filled with food, with hooch instead of blood, he wondered if he really could be held responsible for my shape, or knowing that he couldn't be, was trying to understand the game being played.

Wańka began to laugh, intending to turn everything—and so also the reason for the meeting—into a joke. Father joined him. That's exactly the reaction they had been expecting. I don't really remember what I felt. I sucked my cut finger. If something didn't involve Joachim, I don't really remember it. He was the apple of my eye. The belly button of my world. The tongue of my mouth. The fingerprint of each finger. The edge of my womanhood. My Joachim, my light bearer.

The laughter of Wańka and my father was unexpectedly interrupted by Misza.

"*Heta prauda.*"

"It's still a long way until dawn," Igor remarked.

They sat at the table. The white curtain covered the rectangle of the window glass: it cut the night into a pattern straight from arts and crafts. A pattern that described nothing, folklore from the border, a cutout from tradition. Jozik returned to the *leżajka*. An achoo is binding: he was offended by his mistress. He made this clear by curling into a ball.

Igor felt an unfathomable longing. As if he longed for something he had never tasted, but had already lost. Or longed for continuity, for a thread free of knots rolled onto a ball of wool.

Sonia had reached the part of her story in which her guest had paused to reflect. Sonia carried a child. He didn't know what had happened in her life, but he had gained a certainty, a mistaken certainty, as often happens where certainties are concerned, that the child hadn't left the womb alive.

He tried to imagine the beginning of the show:

. . . he separated the light from the darkness, stupidity from wisdom, the egg from the sperm and ran away . . .

. . . night as bright as day. a sharp light floods the stage. a few white-gray animals approach the window of the house. wolves (these can be the students of theater schools). they raise their muzzles to the ceiling and howl (the howls can come from off-stage). three faces move anxiously in the window. that's when a huge dog with red-tipped fur pounces onto the wooden stage. it's borbus . . .

. . . hunger sucked the stomach. she thought that soon, the end would come. she found some berries under the snow. and then borbus began to bark: a hole with potatoes, hidden in the woods. the owner was probably six feet under by now . . .

. . . he had a son called Wańka, and Wańka had a son called Misza, and Misza had a son called Mikołaj, and Mikołaj will never have a son, or even a dog . . .

"It's true," said Misza (said Sonia). But it wasn't really true. I dropped the dish. Nobody told me off. Father's eyes almost popped: as if he were going to explode, like a mouse strangled by some *hadaść*. Wańka, who had been red for some time, turned a shade of beetroot; only the gray mustache stood out, and the purple veins. I would never have suspected that so many veins could fit in a person's face, like weeds on an untended ridge, couch grass and corn cockle.

Misza momentarily looked grave, but his grave look didn't look serious at all. I didn't know him, but I saw mockery and audacity in his eyes. Maybe it was something else? They say that the eyes don't lie, they also say that what they don't see doesn't hurt anyone. But it does.

Hurt.

My bright Joachim.

It hurts terribly!

Misza rose from the table. He walked over to me, stepping over the shell of the dish. He stood next to me. He placed a hand on my shoulder. This hand seemed heaviest, like a carrying pole. I had never felt such a weight on my shoulder.

"*Heta prauda. My ni znali, jak wam skazać. Ustydna było.*"

Something broke free in me at these words. Or it just broke. I was paying for my own lie and cowardice. I couldn't have thought of a more bitter or cruel truth. My lie had dressed itself in the guise of truth.

I couldn't say a word. I wanted to deny it. I wanted to tell them about Joachim. That I loved only him. It was he, though then he was somewhere far on the eastern front, who was in me. It was him, my bright Joachim.

My heart broke. Not for the first time. That heart broke and broke, it seemed as if the breaking would never stop, like the laying of eggs by a chicken doesn't stop, or pain, or the wilderness, or hunger, or the creaking of floe in winter.

I began to cry. I cried out of self-pity for a long time. When Misza forced me to kneel in front of our fathers. When he kissed my temple. When my brother took me, sobbing, into the yard. When I sat on the bench, and Borbus looked at me and whined quietly. I sat and cried in self-pity. There is more water in a person than blood.

With Joachim there was truth. We didn't know each other's languages, we couldn't lie. Misza and I were joined by a lie. It is a strong glue, too. Not worse than hate. It sticks like a cobweb, taking away freedom and—most importantly—condemns to loneliness. Whom could I tell? Joachim, who wasn't there? Father, who was happy with the turn of events and the bottles of hooch? My brothers? The priest? Who?

I could tell only Misza. I didn't want to. And so, step by step, death by death, month after month—I became increasingly lonely.

The wedding was planned for November. In Królowe Stojło and Słuczanka, in Waliły and Mieleszki, and even in Gródek itself the rumors spread like wildfire. I don't want to recall what was being said, the stories were so unbelievable that even the war paled next to them. It paled, because people in the villages lived life, and war is death. Because people in the villages lived the not-so-distant future, and war is always the present and the past.

For weeks before the wedding, Misza tried to behave as expected, that is: as one should in his position. He visited me every other day, talked to father and my brothers about the yard work and the war, and then we went for a walk to some private place. At first I avoided the places I had visited with Joachim. Then I stopped caring. We sat by the river, and I closed my eyes and looked at Misza. And Misza became Joachim. Joachim changed, as features do with time and distance.

I became so good at lying to myself that I started to look forward to his visits. Because—in a sick way—my walks with

Misza turned out to be walks with Joachim. And Misza didn't interrupt that: he didn't try to touch or kiss me, he didn't ask about anything and said little. He was just there.

Sometimes, somewhere deep, close to the marrow, especially by the river, under the temple, I felt that this was only the imitation of peace, the silence before a shout, a pitchfork in hay. I told myself: better this untruth and imitation than what would happen if you told the truth. That's what I told myself with the stubbornness of a cow trying to ram her way from the barn to a calf being slaughtered in the yard, though I made no effort to try to imagine what might have happened if I hadn't lied.

I remember one such walk. We sat by the river. I remembered Joachim, pale rather than bright, so . . . washed out, further away than the saints from the icons. I looked at Misza and saw only the one at whom I looked: without a trace of Joachim, Misza from line to line.

I looked at him, surprised and scared. I said: "It can't be." I shook my head. "*Heta ni moża być*," I repeated.

"*Musić*," he replied.

Then he started to kiss and touch me. Softly. He must have learned a lot chasing skirts. I didn't defend myself because I didn't find anything worth defending. Because what was there? A fading memory? An unclean innocence? A child?

His touches and kisses gave my body pleasure. Such great pleasure that I grew to hate it. What was this, loving one but letting another love me? Can the heart grow and grow? And the skin answer and answer to a touch?

It was then, by the river, that we consummated our lie. And, what I didn't expect, it didn't kill us. It didn't release us.

It happened.

Sometimes, he found that translating Sonia's thoughts was difficult. Theoretically, it shouldn't be a problem. Their tongues were not that distant, they lived in similar caverns, the same slipperiness, the same ribbed roof of the mouth, the same fear of humiliation. He finds her emotions accessible. Her gender, weakened with age, isn't wholly alien. Nevertheless. Nevertheless, it's not as simple as it might seem to be from the sum of similarities.

He felt more than once that he was removing something valuable from Sonia's story. He felt like a curator in a museum of someone else's memories, like a clockmaker faced with a mechanism taken to pieces. Only when the memories were translated into one's experience did something comprehensible emerge, yet simultaneously it became clear that something else was lost along the way.

Authenticity is, after all, a monstrous film.

I looked beautiful. That's what everyone said, because that's what I was supposed to look like, and what they were supposed to say. I have a picture, in black and white, it survived. It survived because I didn't care for it. I have a white face, black hair, pinned up. I have black lips, eyes of lime and ash. Misza looks better than I remember, though I never wanted to remember what he looked like. I'd prefer it if he was missing a hand and was a hunchback. It wouldn't have made a difference, although—who knows?—it would be easier to think of myself. Not better, but easier. They used to say: if a woman doesn't feel happiness on her wedding day, she won't feel it in her lifetime. I felt happiness before my wedding, and not with the groom.

Once upon a time, at that wedding, far, far away across lifetimes, over many wars and one river, before the Deluge, over the forest that stretched as far as the foreign borders, that ancient day, which struggled against being drowned by the night, I felt fatigue. First, my legs hurt from dancing, then my lips from smiling. I sat down to catch my breath and understood that I was happy. Tied by a lie, but still happy. I didn't want this happiness, I didn't want this contentment with Misza, which was slowly conquering me. Tiny pricks, like mosquito bites or pine needles.

Misza wasn't turning out to be as bad as I wanted him to be. He wasn't atrocious, but handsome. He was the opposite of what I needed to save Joachim within myself.

(Now the actress playing Sonia pauses. She stretches her hands in front of her and folds them into a bird's nest. And then she squeezes them, crushing the hatchlings.)

I could have had a completely different life. A good life. A life that they call good. A home and children. A man beside me for everyone to see. And on the flip side, an old secret, like a postcard from a cousin in America—my bright Joachim. The most radiant.

Yes, I could've had a different life. A good one.

I believed that. I sat on the bench, sweaty, in front of the barn. And I believed that I could have a good life. Ordinary.

(The actress playing Sonia falls silent. A group of tipsy wedding guests appears onstage.)

A barn was built on the stage, the decoration was meant to be symbolic, very literal. The barn completes the function of a location for the wedding reception, somewhere by the walls the echoes of Wyspiański threaten; Polish theater cannot bid goodbye to the corpses, it misses mother and father, father was killed in the Uprising, mother's breasts hurt from milk and her eyes from tears. Tables and benches have been constructed from wooden planks. Sheaves of hay support the walls. The sheaves, of course, resemble mulch stacks.

A conversation between two men

FIRST MAN
Sońka slut.

SECOND MAN
One's afraid to say such things aloud.

FIRST MAN
Sońka slut. She bedded anyone.

SECOND MAN
That's all talk. She went with you?

FIRST MAN
She protested at first. Like a woman, from behind, to warm me up. She protested to encourage me. I satisfied her as a man should, in the back hole, so she could barely walk.
The men chuckle.

A conversation between two women

FIRST WOMAN

So quiet, such a *lelak*. And she swiped Misza right from under our skirts.

SECOND WOMAN

There's no justice.

FIRST WOMAN

There is some of the Lord's justice after all. You'll see. She'll be punished. They always are.

SECOND WOMAN

Who cares if she will be when we'll be old at our fathers' and mothers'?

The women fall silent.

A conversation: a Man, the Groom, and a Voice from offstage.

MAN

Tell the truth, you and Sońka have always? In secret?

GROOM

I always wanted her. And it happened.

MAN

It happens.

GROOM

It does.

MAN

Now what?

GROOM

Now the war.

VOICE FROM OFFSTAGE

The time for small happenings will come yet. But not for you. Not for you. You've already been swept away by the big ones.

There are many days that I won't forget for the rest of my life, that is, until morning, as the fatly shining line of soot is approaching, nipping at my heels. The wedding reception went on and on. The guests fell to the floor, slept, sobered, and fell again. I didn't see the end of this sad wedding. Misza broke someone's nose. They drank, talked, so they fought. Like men. Nothing unusual. I couldn't figure out whose nose didn't stick out anymore, all the noses in sight were red and as if slashed by mosquitoes.

I slipped out of the barn. It was graying. Two German trucks drove down the road. Germans didn't see people unless they were under orders. Very obedient. If any nation can march to heaven and follow the Ten Commandments, it would probably only be them.

(Be careful of stereotypes!—noted Igor.)

I watched the vanishing cars. I watched carelessly.

Then the gray cloud of dust. The dust fell. A motorbike with a third wheel and a cradle. The motorbike stopped. I thought that it was Joachim returning. That he would save me. That he'd take care of me. But whom would he be saving me from? And whom would he be taking care of?

The motorcycle started and disappeared. It went through Słuczanka and turned left, into Królowe Stojło, where I should be. Where I should be, waiting. Today, I don't know if that bike drove down the road, or only in my head. Gray dust and a black motorcyle. My eye was dry, my belly held in tightly by the material. Such a tightly held belly will see many things through the navel. And who can see if I was watching, or being watched?

We moved into a small house, or rather an outhouse, which my father graciously offered. We were to live there until my father-in-law moved to his new house and we could take his old one. I would've preferred to live with my father-in-law. I wouldn't have to see my father and brothers that often. I was convinced, though, and then I convinced Misza. Because if by some twist of fate Joachim would be found, he would be found here, nowhere else.

I told Misza: "*Chaczu paczakać*, we can live with my father." All right, he said, I give you a year to wait, and not a day more. We didn't go back to it again, and a year, it turned out, was too much anyway.

I worked a lot, new chores joined the old ones. My straight-from-the-hell-of-the-Holy-Scriptures parent didn't intend to cheaply hand over the rights to the outhouse that was to be our home for a few months. I worked a lot, and my belly grew. I was endlessly tired and sleep-deprived. First work, then a few hours of sleep, sleep, work, war, sleep, work, fear. On April 2, a child was born, a boy. Bald and ugly. Not similar to Joachim, or to myself, he most resembled dough. And in the village they said: the image of Misza, or of Wańka, of you. I'm not bald, I joked back, I don't have a willy, I joked, and the women laughed, as if they had no worries or backs twisted by work, and dreams full of fear and there was more fear than sand in the yard.

Working and sleeping, not getting in anyone's way and with no time or desire for arguments, I didn't notice when the neighbors changed sides. I stopped being invisible—Misza brought me out of the shadows. I began to be shown certain graces, they didn't spit when they saw me or cross themselves, or cross the road, it was acceptable to chat with me.

We picked a name. Mikołaj. It's a good name. There was a holy miracle worker with that name.

The harsh winter held fast, and when the snows finally melted, it turned out the world was composed of mud. The war forgot us less and less frequently. Contingents, partisans, everyone wanted something, and if they wanted something, they took it. They came and took, first with goodwill, then also with goodwill and a pointed weapon.

How many there were! I couldn't help my surprise, they fought among themselves like ants, and told us that it was for us, that they fought in our name, almost like *Isus*, He also died for us. And what happened then? Why? Never, not in my lifetime, have so many fought in the name of so few. In times of war various plagues befall people, we got one too. An excess of defenders.

What should have been growing in me was love for Mikołaj, what did grow was hatred toward father. I blamed him for everything that didn't go the way I wanted, *u buchtu. W pizdu*. I blamed him for my lies. For the fallen barn. For the dead calf. For the martens in the chicken coop.

Misza waited a month after Mikołaj's birth before fulfilling his marital duties, which I didn't discourage him from, I must admit. I was returning to the land of the living from some faraway place, as if from a long and devastating illness, from beyond some glaucoma, like an insect seen through the bottom of a bottle. I worked more than I had to, to deserve a deep sleep. It happened that I hummed to Mikołaj. It happened that I laughed. It happened that I brushed Borbus's fur until it shone. It happened that I gossiped with the women.

It happened that I would touch Misza's unshaven cheek with my hand. It happened that I would run my fingers through his hair. It happened that I would even be angry with him for some made-up mistake.

It happened.

After the difficult success of *Królowe Stojło*, Igor decided to learn Sonia's story in even more detail. Sonia was already dead. But death doesn't stand in the way of finding out about someone's life. Using a variety of sources and connections, he was able to determine who Joachim was.

Joachim Castorp, a devastatingly meaningful name, born on July 26, 1913 in Gdańsk. The only child of well-connected parents. His father was a lawyer, his mother was famous—which was quite common in those times among well-off city folk—for her parapsychological abilities; it was probably thanks to these that a large part of the fortune could be moved abroad, even before the war. For reasons unknown Joachim gave his life to the new rule, he burned with love for the Third Reich and its leaders. It led to a conflict with his parents, solid city folk, doubtful that the extermination of any race might provide solid fundaments for a happier, richer way of life. It's likely that Joachim saw his parents for the last time in 1937. His father died a year later. His mother survived the war.

Joachim was wounded in 1942. The documents don't specify where or how. Certain leads allow for the suspicion that it might have happened in a village in Podlasie. It's only known that recovery didn't take long, and afterward Joachim disappeared from the medical records. In 1944, probably because of his mother's interference, he managed to make his way to Switzerland. From there, in a roundabout way, to Central America. He changed his name and his past.

First, he made profit in sugarcane, then cacao, coffee, and finally bananas and pineapples. And tourism. He never married. He died, in full command of his mental faculties, in 2003. He had no heirs. He gave his fortune to a charity fighting for animal rights. He must have lost faith in people.

Nothing else could be determined. Igor didn't find out

much about Joachim. He turned out to be resourceful, firstly. And—secondly—he survived the war, though Sonia claimed otherwise.

It was said that the war wouldn't last long now. The Germans were losing, it didn't make a difference to me at all. Joachim wasn't there, neither was Misza, or Mikołaj. Janek and Witek weren't there, neither was father. Many of the neighbors weren't there. The only absence that made me happy was father's. The longer he wasn't there though, the less I knew how to be happy. A person can only be happy because of what they have, not because of what they don't have, unless they are *Palak*; they are different, but there aren't many of them among us, they multiplied only after the war. Where did they all come from if they'd supposedly all died in the uprisings and the war?!

Only the cat Wasyl and two cows, Zorka and Malina, were left from the old days, and Borbus. Borbus grew larger than other dogs. Larger than a calf, I couldn't feed him well anymore, we weren't in the best situation with food. Nettle soup, *kaluczki* caught in the river, fish not much larger than the nail of an old hag. We ate everything that could fill the belly. And Borbus grew and grew. As if he fed on lack, as if every death gave him strength and size. Borbus managed to catch a hare a few times and bring it home. It was like a Holy Day. Because those weren't icons and aspergillum anymore, but real meat.

I think September started. The Germans unexpectedly surrounded Słuczanka and Królowe Stojło. They weren't after anything specific. They probably received the order to kill as many as they could, saving bullets if possible. Most managed to hide or escape. Those who had no luck or hiding places were chased out of their homes and onto the road. There was a truck standing by the bridge. They ordered us onto it. I was the last one, separate from the group, because I had limped ever since

Joachim's death, that's why they called me Sońka *Kulhawa*. I thought that if I got in the truck, they would kill me. I didn't want to wait for death. I lost everything that I wanted and I wanted to have this over and done with as quickly as possible, that is—life.

That's why I started to run toward the bushes by the river. I managed to run away because some commotion started, but I don't remember, besides, the Germans didn't expect insubordination. They are a very proper nation—when it comes to dying and killing, they die and kill. If the Russians were equally proper, they would've lost the war in the blink of an eye.

I grew afraid that I'd survive. *Ihnat*, imagine how pitiful my escape was. I, the only limping person in two villages, running to the river, or rather, limping there. And the Germans noticed quite late, a neighbor from Słuczanka pointed me out. The Germans began to yell, and I, despite wanting to live, because a person always wants to live, even when they think they've lost everything and there is nothing to wait for, I ran, the only one to run.

(Lot's wife, Igor noted; what a pity it's an association we can't use.)

That's when Borbus leaped at the German. I don't know where he came from. The Germans shot twice. I screamed once. The bullets: one with my name, the other with an insult, hit my dog. They died together. My beloved Borbus and the German soldier with his throat ripped out. That's why I got away. Running, I didn't think I might regret something. I forgot about my dog. Borbus saved me.

I always found someone to cry over. We didn't see anyone who was taken away on the truck. Apparently, they were ordered to dig a deep pit past Waliły, then their hands and legs were tied, and they were thrown alive into the pit. Then, it was covered up. The earth moved, worms churned the soil. Then grass and birches grew. Then we forgot. Or maybe none of them existed? They were never here?

I sat in the bushes for the whole day. Only in the evening was I brave enough to glance at the road. I found Borbus's body. The Germans left it as it had fallen. I went to the hut. I found a wheelbarrow and moved the body with it. In the yard, close to the chicken coop, I dug a deep pit. It was night, I barely saw anything. I tripped and fell into the pit. I knew that nobody would help me. There was nobody left. I knew that the war would end soon, because there were barely any people. They died. And when there are no people, there is no war.

I got out of the pit in the morning. My hip was on fire. The chickens were pecking at Borbus's body. Borbus's body had stiffened, but its eye—open—wasn't matte. Its tongue had gone purple, it spilled out from behind its teeth like a *lizun*. Blood clots. It was the German soldier's blood. It didn't look any different than my dog's blood. They taught me that a man is worth more than an animal. Blood didn't confirm this. Borbus was more than a man. I took off his collar. I pushed his body. I covered it with earth. I sat on the pile of moved soil.

I would have sat there until the war ended if it wasn't for the cows. One had to go into the forest, milk them, because though hidden, it was as clear as if they were visible that they needed milking. So I went. I limped.

And when I came back—I was gone a long time—the Russians had arrived. The Poles. They said that it would be better than before the war. Nobody believed them. There was nobody to believe. Those that could have were a long time gone. And those that arrived soon went on to repeat their fairy tales.

Long, long ago. One would prefer not to remember, not to hear, one would prefer to join the absent ones. If someone is dead, does that mean they once were real? Or not anymore? Never?

There was no longer night than the one Sonia spent with her guest. The fourth hut in Królowe Stojło is not just a hole in cell reception, not only a gap in the dataset of the Central Statistics Office, not only *baciuszka*'s wasted petrol money for the valuable pagoda and, like a pagoda, persisting by the road, Daewoo Espero (*espero* like *ira*, a Spanish word, though it means something quite the opposite).

Because the fourth hut in Królowe Stojło is also a singularity, and inside every singularity time passes differently, other things appeared like waves in the ocean, and bones disappeared into sand. Years broke against people. Ignacy aged, Sonia grew younger, Igor stayed silent, and she could soon pass for the daughter of her guest.

Because in the fourth hut in Królowe Stojło the end met the beginning, death with birth, past with future, and both weighed out with pouches of ash. Apparently in the row of icons in Deesis, written paintings stretched out: twelve dogs called Borbus with gothic collar aureolas, nine cats with green eyes that, where the shadow from the olive lamps fell, gave the impression of staring.

And great was the happiness in the fourth hut of Królowe Stojło. Sonia was joyous because she was leaving in glory.

I am Sonia the White, I am Sonia the Cripple, I am the last like my bitch Borbus the Twelfth, like my cat Jozik the Mouse Shepherd, the last of a line am I, my blood was wiped from this world during the war, after that it was only drying up. I am from Królowe Stojło, where proud kings rested, I am from the Trochimczyk house, I am a mother whose child was killed, I am a sister whose brothers were killed, I am a daughter whose father was killed, I am a wife whose husband was killed, I am a lover whose lover was killed, a neighbor with no neighbors, despair with no vocal chords, a complaint with no confessor, a confession with no forgiveness.

(The actress sits on a bench on the right side of the stage. She peels potatoes. She takes them from a basket and throws them into a bucket.)

I am Misza, I have a surname, I had parents and brothers, I had a wife and a son, a business, two horses had I, nine cows, and in the Orthodox church I had a place right by St. Mikołaj himself. I had a handsome face, hard muscles, and a large penis. I had plans. A head and hands. Everything in its place. And now I have a grave in the woods. I don't have a body in that grave. Animals scattered my body.

(The actor who plays Misza sits next to Sonia. Peeled potatoes fall into the empty bucket with a clatter.)

I am Ignacy, I am performing in third-person. I am performing accidentally, I perform in front of myself. I sit in the last row, or maybe I am lying in bed. It depends on the night. I am the guardian of this tale. Its risky director and temporary hero. The producer and historian. I will be the last to leave this theater or I will go to the all-night store. It depends on the night, whether I'm in the last row or lying in bed, waiting for insomnia.

(The actor playing Ignacy sits next to Sonia and Misza.)

I was peeling potatoes. On the bench in front of the hut. It was warm and dry. Quiet. Borbus lay curled into a ball. Wasyl was warming himself on the stone. Father and my brothers were in the fields. Misza was helping my father-in-law. Mikołaj was asleep, he drank the milk from one breast and made a face at the other. I was peeling potatoes. I was thinking about fish. I craved fish. I thought about the hole in the sheepskin coat. It needed patching.

And then, long, long ago, in the least appropriate moment, Joachim returned. I was waiting for him. That's true. I waited for him not in order for my waiting to end, though; I waited for him not to return. For his skin to cool, like my memories had. For his eyes to reach no higher than my ankles, so I wouldn't drown in them.

I waited for the waiting never to end. And yet: he stood before me. I saw the tips of dusty shoes. It was also August. In the previous August juices pulsed, and in this one, long, long ago, the throat dried up, before the Deluge.

I wasn't sitting there in my best dress. I was sitting in a mottled gray caftan. I wasn't dressed up, only a little tired. I was damaged and worked to the bone. Calloused and thin. I saw the tips of dusty shoes and the potatoes fell from my hands. They rolled over the compact earth. I didn't dare lift my head, and Joachim didn't dare touch my face. Borbus brought a potato in his teeth. He pushed it into my hand and wagged his tail, waiting for a reward.

Joachim knelt. He took the *bulwa* from the doggy's mouth. He stroked the dog. Then he read the silver letters on the collar.

"Borbus," he said.

Borbus barked happily. I didn't say anything.

"*Zu spät?*" he asked.

I understood. I didn't know how to answer. In any language.

Because how to say—that it's too late but also too early? That he didn't let me live because he wasn't there, and that now he was killing me because he was? How to say all that? How to answer? How?

That's when Mikołaj cried. I left him in the crib in the entryway. Mikołaj was crying louder and louder. I should get up and give him my other breast. But I couldn't have held a knife, much less a child. Mikołaj cried.

Joachim got up and walked into the entryway. Nobody invited him, but he still went inside, as Germans do. The child fell silent. Joachim came back with Mikołaj in his arms. Mikołaj was babbling. Saying something. Maybe that's what German children do, because I didn't understand anything, and Joachim understood everything. They talked like father and son. Like blood with blood, like a cricket with seeds.

Moj Hospadzi, I couldn't even look at them. I sat over the bucket, scattered potatoes like a holy aureola, my calloused hands like empty bowls, and the caftan like a *pakrowa*.

Joachim knelt.

"*Danke, vielen Dank*," he said like that, or differently—it's not up to me to decide what he said.

He touched me. Also his words. His hand touched me. I could smell the wax of the seal that *Boh* used to join our lives. That seal, cream and strawberries, honeycomb of bees and incense, sin and wine, mother's skirts and a star from heaven.

He touched me. And I understood: Sońka, you lift your eyes and you die. Sońka, you look and you kill. You lift your eyes, Sońka, and you kill everyone, I understood. That August was the beginning. This August will be the end, if you lift your eyes.

If.

You.

Lift.

Your.

Eyes.

I squeezed my eyes shut. I wanted Joachim to put Mikołaj down: in the cradle, among the potatoes, anywhere. I wanted him to leave. I wanted him never to have come in the first place. I never wanted him to leave. I squeezed my eyes shut.

I squeezed my eyes shut.

I squeezed my eyes shut so tightly that I should have smothered them, but they persisted. My eyelids fluttered. They weakened, but they were alive, like fish on sand.

How long could I stop myself for? Whom could I lean on?

I can't name it. Just imagine, *Ihnat*, that the person you love more than life itself returns. And you understand what "more than life itself" means. That it isn't your life at all. That the "more than life itself" is the life of your husband, your son, your family.

I squeezed my eyes shut. Out of terror. I'd never felt such terror. I was afraid that I would lose, that I would look at him. I was afraid. I was afraid for myself, for Joachim, for my relatives, for time. I was so afraid that my eyelids were covered with a pall. I fell from the bench, I might have vomited.

When I opened my eyes, I stumbled across his face. I knew it was the end. I felt some sort of relief. It happened. It couldn't unhappen. Nothing was up to me anymore. I tried. I tried as hard as I could. I didn't lie.

When I opened my eyes, I stumbled across his face, like a wall, with impact. He'd aged in the time we didn't see each other. His eyes were huge, he'd lost weight, and in those eyes I saw myself. Not myself in the mottled gray caftan, ragged plait, and flat eyes.

When I opened my eyes, I stumbled across his face.

He'd changed, but nothing had changed.

When I opened my eyes, it was all over.

Sonia fell silent. She looked at her guest over the table covered with an oilcloth. She looked with one eye the color of blue tiles, and the other—gray and matte like a fieldstone. Sonia looked at Ignacy, who had shaken Igor off for good, at least in that moment he returned to his real name, the first one from his grandparents, from here to nowhere. She looked with the night's eye, like a moth that can't see but is aiming toward the source of the glow, which is the spring of death. Responsibility was taken from her, her itinerary was set, her honors had been bidden farewell, she had had her last anointment, a volley of shots had been fired in salute, though she was still alive, the place on the oilcloth had been pointed out, the place where she would fall with her wings dustless, with signs of ash. Ash can fly, too.

"You disappeared," Ignacy said. "You disappeared."

For the first and last time, Ignacy spoke to Sonia in the second person. It is this moment in the story that decides everything. It is this moment that divides life between a before and an after, into a long time and long ago, but most importantly into never and never again.

"*Ja prapała. Prapała.*"

Sonia closed her eyes. Her eyelids fluttered. As if fighting a battle from decades earlier. A battle ended, survived, measured out, written down. And punished, though justice is not a human word.

I couldn't stop. I looked at Joachim. I swam in the water of his eyes. I touched the soil of his skin. He was thinner and aged. He was half-kneeling over me. It happened. It happens. It happened.

I submerged myself into every wrinkle, I tripped over skin discolorations, I stepped over a swollen vein on the temple, I followed individual gray hairs, the vertical lines on the forehead, sudden crow's feet in the corners of his eyes, dry lips.

And then I started to cry.

It happened. It happens.

I was like a bottomless well, like a dark and deep well, like wild meat growing against and in spite of, I cried and cried. I had someone to cry over. A row of graves. Joachim lay next to me. He embraced me.

I knew that everything came back. There was no salvation. No explanation. I loved Joachim. I loved him beyond all measure. I loved him more than Mikołaj's life, Misza's, my brothers'.

When he touched me, when he breathed into my skin, when he directed my hand along the line of his spine, small vertebra after vertebra, crusts of lust when he was nearby, the smell of the lumber mill—I disappeared, and simultaneously I was more real and bodily than ever.

My Joachim, bright Joachim, the pupil of my soul, the heat of my loins, the aureola of my saints, the curse of my loved ones. My Joachim. My golden Joachim. Joachim speaking in foreign tongues and opening me up to tremble. Spasms which sped along a string that sounded only near him.

We lay beside each other. I cried from happiness and unhappiness. I felt what a hero of a story feels when it's ending. I knew that this ending would be terrible, that I probably wouldn't even make it to the end. I knew. But before the ending came, we still had a few paragraphs. Happy ones, because he found me. Because we appeared in sentences together.

We lay beside each other like in a painting. Motionless. He and I. Mikołaj between us, asleep now. In the background there was soil, with patches of grass. My gray caftan and his black uniform. Borbus and Wasyl. Silver letters and a double lightning bolt.

We lay beside each other, and slowly I calmed down. I knew that there was nothing I could do anymore.

It happened. Happens.

We lay beside each other like apples that fall from the apple tree, but this time nobody discovered anything.

Sonia was silent. If the minutes of her life were counted, it would probably turn out that she was silent for most of her life. That the companions of her conversations were cows, a cat, and a dog. A field, a river, and household objects. She sits now, with eyes of different colors, young and pink, slender as an aspen, fresh as sheets gathered from the wind. She is approaching the end of her own life. She is approaching the end of the story. She takes a ball of material. Dried forget-me-nots and strings of cotton. A dark stain of blood. The old one, from the stories, and the new one, from Ignacy's nose, though Igor probably dripped some too.

The threads of fabric and flower stems come alive under the touch of her skin. Sonia sits on the *leżajka* with a bouquet of flowers. Fragile blue petals with a yellow, smoldered eye in the middle. Jozik the Mouse Shepherd grudgingly moves over for his mistress. He avoids the tears: a grain of salt and fieldstone. Jozik stretches his own body into a crippled omega with patches of fur and a mouth with holes left over from fangs. He jumps onto the table. Looks through the window. Two hits with a paw are like two clicks of a mouse: close the icon and also: confirm.

Jozik hits the window twice. Night beyond the window, a black rectangle in a white frame. Night beyond the window, which turns to day at the second hit. Jozik narrows his eyes. Pupils narrow, no wider than two daggers, staring into the day like the pupils of a goat. Into the rays of sunshine.

Joachim left. I knew that we would meet the next day. I did what I had to do. In the night Misza wanted to make love. I gave myself to him, because the only thing I had enough of for everyone was my body. My heart, burning and taken. And my husband wasn't a bad man. He shared everything with me. He even shared my lie. My husband wasn't a bad man.

Misza lay on top of me. Steady breaths warmed my right ear. I thought he'd fallen asleep. I thought that this night was our goodbye. I whispered: "*Czamu ty mnie uział, czamu?*" It wasn't a question. It was an accusation and a thank you. I thought he was asleep.

He wasn't asleep. I felt his muscles tighten.

"*Jon wiarnutsa,*" he said. "*Jon wiarnutsa znou,*" he said. And his *znou* sounded in my ear, in his warm breath, like *krou*.

Onstage, a large bed with snowy sheets. On the bed, two people: the actors playing Sonia and Misza. They lie in an embrace. A heavy purple material is in the background, surrounding the bed in a half-circle, like a curtain or a war. The bed is arranged in such a way that the audience gets the impression of looking down on Sonia and Misza. As if they were floating in air, as if they can pass judgments, though it's only a stage trick. The First Scene of Awakening.

SONIA
Why did you take me in? Why?

MISZA
He came back. He's back again.

Sonia doesn't answer.

Say the name of the father of our child.

Sonia doesn't answer.

Say it. I never asked for anything. Now I do. Say it.

SONIA
Joachim.

MISZA
Joachim.

After a longer pause.

What's he like?

SONIA
Fiery.

Misza is silent.

Why did you lie?
Why did you save me?

MISZA
For me you are the fiery one.

The actor says this line as if in spite of himself; if he's not workshop proficient, he should talk through his teeth.

Your lie was like an answer to a prayer.
I got what I wanted, I thought.
The heavens spread out beneath my feet.

SONIA
That's enough. Don't speak.

MISZA
Do you remember, four years ago in Gródek we buried my mother.
Do you remember?

Sonia is silent.

I know you remember.
You remember years ago, long, long ago, at the cemetery in Gródek you came up to me. You were wearing your best dress. The one with the blue flowers. It was your only decent dress, it could be let out as you grew, you had nothing darker, nothing more appropriate. That's why you wore such a happy dress to a funeral.

I loved my mother very much. I stood over the grave with my love, unneeded, stupidly large. Mother was gone. Love stayed. It weighed downward. Like every love does, sooner or later. No love ends up in heaven, always in the earth. Earth.

That's when you came up to me in the flowery dress. You touched my shoulder and you said something. I don't know what you said because you touched me. When you touched me it was like a bolt of lightning erupted in me.

I know you remember. You don't forget something like that.

Something exploded in me. It shook my entire body.

I felt enormous joy and enormous sadness. And everything came from your touch.

I understood that I was lost. That *Boh* joined our lives with a seal. I smelled the wax of that seal, the smell of churned earth and flowers, incense and sweat, cold water and bacon.

I understood that I was lost when I looked into your eyes. Your gray fieldstones. Every day when I wake I have in front of me your gray fieldstones. For four years. For four years I've seen your eyes after waking, and only after that the sun; stones and then light. Such is my fate.

SONIA
Don't speak.
Don't speak.
The shame.

MISZA
I understood that I was lost. I don't have control over myself. I was brave enough to put my hand on your hand on my shoulder. And then I waited. I waited for something to join us. That the wax didn't smell for nothing. I waited for almost four years.

When you lied, the heavens opened up for me. I could feel your hand on my shoulder again. We kneeled before our fathers.

We owned up to love. You were silent, I didn't have to be.

I was only confirming what had happened at the cemetery in Gródek. What I had waited for for so many years.

I knew that you had some German. Everyone knew. They wanted to shave your head, rape you, kill you. I defended you. I told them that I would kill whoever touched you.

That's why everyone believed in our love so easily. Everyone, Sońka, everyone knew that you were my whole world. That's why they believed it so easily. Your father and mine. Everyone knew except you. Everyone. Except you.

I didn't expect anything. I mean, I did expect that you'd grow to return my feelings, in time. I couldn't comprehend with heart or mind how you might not. Because how could you, my whole world, deny me?

I waited patiently. After so many years one learns how to wait. Knows how to wait. I waited.

I found happiness. I woke up beside you. That's a lot already. I slept with you. That's a lot. The most, though: sometimes you looked at me, looked with the gray fieldstones, and I knew you were looking at me. Not at that German, but at me. Sometimes you'd touch my cheek. Sometimes you smoothed my hair.

These are small things, they weigh more than vows.

Tell me, is he, this Joachim, better than me?

SONIA
Miszka . . .

MISZA
I'm glad we're talking. I'm talking. It was a weight to bear. Now you'll have to bear it too. I know you will. You will, because the other one is everything to you. For him you'll bear anything. I'm telling you because it weighed on me. I'm telling you so you know that I understand you.

I can't hold it against you, though I do a little. I know that you can't help it. You can't, but I still hate him.

I'd kill him! But if I raised my hand to him, it would be like raising my hand to you. And if I killed you, I'd be killing myself. That's a sin.

Sin.

A situation with no escape.

SONIA
I'm with you.

MISZA
What?

SONIA
I'm with you.
That's what I said at the cemetery, long ago.

The First Scene of Awakening. According to Igor, it was one of the most beautiful scenes in *Królowe Stojło*. He didn't watch it often. It caused him a lot of pain. He envied Misza that he loved. He envied Sonia that she loved and was loved.

If Igor had been anyone other than a director, he'd have ordered Sonia to understand that Joachim was an illusion, that Misza was happiness. Igor wished he could correct it, make the final change, even against the wishes of his heroes.

If he had any real power to influence the lives of his characters, the curtain would fall after Sonia's words: "I'm with you."

But this isn't, unfortunately, for fuck's sake, the final scene, he thought.

For the first and last time, it turned out, Misza and I really talked. We talked late into the night. My husband talked most of all. I talked little. I didn't have to. It was a necessary conversation. After this conversation I felt heavier, because Misza got out what was weighing him down, and lighter, because what I was hiding out in the open that night. I slept deeply. I don't think he slept. We lay in an embrace. Closely. The sweat from our bodies mixed and stuck them together like honey sticks to fingers. Lips to lips, we didn't know if it was sleep already or maybe the final kiss; we breathed into one another, lips like a layer cake—his lip, breath, mine, breath, his lip, breath, mine, war.

Because my husband is a good man. He was a good man. Maybe I wouldn't have walked through fire for him, but I definitely would have gotten a bucket of water to douse it. I could have tied myself to him. Think of him. Miss him. Who knows?

If we'd had another few years, I think we would have had a good life. An ordinary, toilsome, good life. In the best color—gray, but the kind of gray that spring arrives in, that the river blues in summer, and choir singers clown around in in winter.

The next day, Sunday. We rose in the morning. We were supposed to go to the Orthodox church. *Da Haradka*. I thought about confession. What would I tell the priest and *Boh*? That my husband forgave my sins, so *Boh* should do so too? That I confessed already and didn't need to do so again? That He could stick the prosphoron up his ass or hide it in His beard for a rainy day?

I did what had to be done in the yard. I heated water. We washed ourselves. I put on my best dress, the one with forget-me-nots. Father harnessed the horses. We didn't get far, over the bridge to the crossroads: Słuczanka to the right, an empty country road to the left, and straight—to Gródek.

We didn't get far. There were two Germans at the crossroads. A motorcycle and a truck stood next to them. And more soldiers, further on. There wasn't enough space to turn around. But even if we'd tried, the Germans would've grown interested in us, and this way there was a shadow of a chance they'd just wave us through.

We didn't get far. Everyone was afraid. Father squeezed the reins. I held Mikołaj tightly. Janek and Witek tensed, curled their hands into fists, and looked at the pitchfork at the bottom of the cart. Only Misza seemed calm. He put a hand on the back of my neck and massaged lightly, as he would a boar when he searched for its balls to cut them off.

We didn't get far, when I noticed Joachim standing with the group of soldiers. The Germans who were sitting or standing on the crossroads stopped the cart. They ordered us off. They drew their guns from their holsters. I got off, hugging Mikołaj to my breast. I was afraid, my legs and hands were afraid, my lungs and my heart, my breasts and womanly place. I wet myself out of fear, though I should have dried up. I was all cotton and terror, goose down pulled from the skin with blood. Misza wanted to get off after me, they didn't let him.

I stood like that, waiting on trembling legs, a trembling poplar and mimosa. And a reed cut down by the first frost. Joachim said something, the soldiers laughed. Then Joachim turned and walked over to me. His companion, younger than Joachim, approached the cart and offered everyone a cigarette. Mine accepted and lit them, though nobody smoked usually, not father, not my brothers, not Misza. I didn't understand anything. I was afraid. Fear doesn't have to be understood.

Joachim stopped in front of me. I saw in his eyes that he'd been waiting for me, that he was happy to see me. And I thought, before he even touched me, that he didn't understand anything, he didn't know about my husband, he wasn't aware in front of whose eyes this scene was unfolding.

I couldn't know what he wanted. Maybe he wanted to save me and take me with him? Free me? But for God's sake, don't have him free me from my husband in front of my husband, from my family in front of my family!

Joachim stopped in front of me. The soldiers talked in hushed voices. The men on the cart smoked cigarettes, though nobody smoked usually. I hugged Mikołaj to my breast. I regretted, I regretted so much that I didn't speak Joachim's tongue. That I couldn't warn myself or him.

Joachim stopped in front of me. Mikołaj cried. Joachim said something. I didn't understand. Mikołaj cried louder. Joachim stretched out his arms toward the child.

And then everything happened so quickly.

So quickly.

Before I handed the child over to Joachim, Witek jumped from the cart. And Misza. Witek was holding the pitchfork. He was faster. Always dopey, but that one time he was faster. Before Joachim touched his son, Witek pushed the pitchfork through Joachim.

Witek pushed the pitchfork through Joachim. Dopey his entire life, but this one time he was faster than the others, faster. Joachim lost his balance and fell on me.

We flew backwards, onto my back, together, all flat. The wrong way round. The family that never was. Father, mother, and son. And the pitchfork.

One time, he was faster. Everyone started shouting. And running. And shooting.

Witek ran, he didn't run far. The bullet was faster. One time, he was faster, and then dopey once again. The bullet was faster. It didn't have to rush.

Father ran. He ran and he ran away. Our *Haspodź* allows the unworthy a long life.

Janek ran. He ran and he ran away. They killed him later. Three weeks later, as if in the next moment.

Misza got to us. He ripped the gun from Joachim's holster. Then he ran. Everything happened so quickly. Misza ran and ran away.

And we lay there. Joachim lay on top of me and Mikołaj. A soldier ran up to us. Everything happened so quickly. He tugged. He pulled the pitchfork out. A wet sound. So quickly. A wet sound and a crack, like a rooster's head falling onto a stone, beak first.

That sound. I'll never forget it. I dream of it. I dream of it, and I can't wake myself up or deafen myself. I hear it when I sleep. I hear it whenever I see *wiły*. I hear it in the Orthodox church.

That sound. As if someone were knocking a calf unconscious with a stone. A slap against water. And a crunch, muffled by meat. Plask.

A soldier ran up to us. Everything happened so quickly. He tugged. He pulled the pitchfork out. I felt warmth on my stomach. And lower.

Joachim's eyes were fading. When the soldier tugged, to pull out the pitchfork, Joachim lifted himself slightly. For a second maybe, then he fell on me. And Mikołaj. Like a pile of rags. I felt warmth on my stomach. And lower.

It wasn't a good, dry warmth, like from over the *plita*. It wasn't a good, damp warmth, like with a man. It was warmth that was heavy and thick, sticky. Foreign. Like heated wax or metal.

I felt heat on my stomach. And lower. Everything happened so quickly. And Witek, who was faster one time too few, one time too many. And Janek, who ran and ran away, straight under the lid of a coffin. And father . . . so fast.

Foreign. Heavy. Sticky.

Joachim's eyes faded, his face like a cloth, so white, lips white, only a red line from his lips, first one and then a second, red like ribbons, I'd have tied them into the bow of a tourniquet to stop him from dying. To stop him, anything but this. Not now and not ever. Never.

Foreign—that's what Joachim's blood was, though his body was so familiar. Heavy—that's what Joachim's blood was, though he himself weighed little, he'd lost so much weight.

The soldiers lifted Joachim's body. They tried to stop the bleeding, shouting nervously, I knew it was all pointless. That I wouldn't see him again. That too much life had escaped through the holes left by the pitchfork. So quickly.

So much life escaped so quickly.

I lay there like a field of blue flowers. With a purple pond. I wasn't allowed to lie for long. Mikołaj was next to me. He was whimpering. Another soldier came up to us. With his gun out. Before anything, he had already shot at Mikołaj. Maybe I could have loved my son more, I could have loved more, he was from me, but even more from Joachim, but there wasn't enough time. Too quickly. So quickly.

And the soldier wanted to shoot at me, but the gun jammed, and his companion was tugging his weapon away. They fumbled.

The companion tugged the gun away from the soldier. He was yelling something I didn't understand. All of this was happening too quickly and not in my language. He tugged his gun away, but he didn't take off his heavy boots. A bullet would have been faster. Boots were heavier and closer.

The soldier, the disarmed one, kicked me. A bone crunched. I lost consciousness. Quickly. But too slowly. Too slowly. Too slowly.

Sonia sat on the *leżajka*. An ordinary *leżajka* of beige tiles. In an ordinary kitchen with an ordinary table. In an ordinary, dark checkered caftan. With ordinary, though fake, teeth in her gums, which were also ordinary. In an ordinary world without marching troops, without words shouted with a capital letter, without W-hour and other cemeteries.

She told of her ordinary life, sitting in a place where people didn't live for long enough, because history tangled them in the spokes of its wheel, and history is always against people. History is always against people, and most of all—women.

Sonia, suddenly so young, with a bouquet of forget-me-nots in her hands and a scarlet ribbon, sat in silence. She remembered what she had lived through, and imagined what she would live through when she died. Or rather: with whom. And that "nothing" is a good word. Bringing relief, like a compress of vinegar after the sting of a wasp.

Time. Her time was ending.

Igor was also silent, pushed inside himself since childhood, pushed out of Warsaw, he was silent like the pedantic secretary of an editorial board. Igor respected Sonia, and it's only right we should respect Igor, because he was the one who bid goodbye to Sonia White, Sonia Crippled, Sonia of the Twelve Dogs, Nine Cats, and Numerous Pains. It's only right to respect him, though it's also all right to dislike him, or to hold him in contempt. Why not?

He sat on the cobblestones, in the middle of the brick cross-roads. He didn't open his eyes. The cigarette was burning away between his fingers.

Igor developed this habit soon after the show's opening night. He went into the countryside whenever his career allowed him to, far away from Warsaw, and he sat there, where what he was trying to show had happened.

Here, exactly here, was where the Second Scene of Awakening had happened. He had watched it many times. On the planks of the stage, three bodies lay. Sonia lay like a trampled field of blue flowers. Witek lay like a felled tree. Mikołajek lay like a red bundle or broken egg with a chick in a cradle of eggshells. Exactly here. There lay three bodies and one person.

Igor sat with closed eyes and a cigarette. He wondered what else could be improved. The cobblestones weren't freezing his ass off anymore. They hurt, but their hardness is, he's not sure what, calming. Sonia moans quietly. It's a single moan. The awakening of a body. The actor playing Ignacy puts on his wings. The wings are made of glue, plastic, and real goose feathers. They will last for many wars and shows, wings aren't worn down so quickly, so rarely used, almost new, trudging on the ground is more likely than waving in the air. Those wings won't be worn away by flight, maybe chlorine, which was used to whiten them. Because whitening, as opposed to flying, happens often—this world is dirty even after the rain.

I'm Gabryiel Nineteenth, that's the role I was cast in, I'm the Guardian Angel, or rather the janitor. I mainly clean. I lift the red bundle. This bundle consists of material, meat, bones, and a single bullet. This bundle was, going back by a quarter of an hour, a bullet and five pages, Mikołajek.

I head toward the side of the road with the bundle. The earth is soft. I have to dig a pit. Not a large one. I don't like to dig, that's why I picked Mikołajek, and not Witek. Witek is large, the pit would have to be deep, and I only have my own hands and a pitchfork, the whims of my Boss.

I work in the sweat of my brow. Angels have no gender, they have foreheads, they have no blood, but they have sweat in excess; I dig with my hands, I churn the earth with the pitchfork. I try not to get dirt on my wings.

The pit's been dug, not very deep, not very wide, just right. I'm Gabryiel Nineteenth, I clean and guard. Nobody is expecting me to overwork myself or stay silent.

I kiss the bundle. I bless it, though I have no such power. Then I cover it with earth. And I think to myself that my place is on the top of a pin, and not here, at the crossroads, from which every road leads toward evil and sadness. This world is disgusting, and only rarely does somebody wonderful happen. This world could be supported by photosynthesis, but it's supported by the spilling of blood. And they teach us on blue sets. They have to teach, because cruelty cannot be understood. They teach us that the most right and only religion is misanthropy broken by empathy and compassion. That's all that's left after crossing the boundary beyond photosynthesis. Only that.

And I thought that I would stick the pitchfork in the ground next to Sonia. She'll find it useful.

Pain woke me. A dull, pulsing pain in my hip, like an abscess in a tooth after a swig of freezing water. I raised myself on my elbows with difficulty. There wasn't a living soul anywhere in sight. The first few hovels in Słuczanka. Nearby, Witek's body, twisted strangely, like a cabbage leaf rolled along by bugs. There were no Germans, no motorcycle or truck. There was no Joachim. There was no Mikołaj. There was no cart. Someone had left the pitchfork tip-first in the ground, nearby, by the road.

I remembered what had happened. I remembered also that it couldn't have happened. Because to what end? Why? Events shouldn't happen without reason. That's a sin.

Pain woke me. A dull, pulsing pain in my hip, I raised myself on my elbows with difficulty. I woke up, and there wasn't a living soul anywhere in sight, and the dead ones were blurry. That's why I thought I was only just falling asleep, that I'm falling into sleep. Because how else to explain the emptiness around? The stones on which I was lying? The brown stain on my dress? The lack of my child and husband? Joachim's absence?

Because I was dreaming, as it happens in dreams, I couldn't force my body to obey me. I couldn't force my body to rise up, because the sky was hanging over my face, so close that I had to breathe through it, too close, like a wet cloth. It leaned on the pitchfork handle, and then fell like a damp, heavy sheet, to stop over Witek's twisted body.

I looked around me. I decided to crawl to the pitchfork, because the sky was hanging higher up there, as if drier and lighter; perhaps I'd be able to stand up that way? That's what I thought, in this dream or the other. I knew that it wasn't real. I didn't want to waste real tears on an unreal world. I was afraid that the real tears would change my nightmare into reality. That's why I crawled, bit by bit, and despite that I didn't cry, stone by stone, I didn't cry, not even the smallest grain of gravel.

Finally, I reached the pitchfork. I don't know how long it took. I looked over my shoulder. I saw a mottled trail, shining like the fluid that a snail uses to mark its way. The trail was very clear; a snail carries its house on its back. And I? I had a stained dress on my back. Such a dress is appropriate for outings, for Sundays. It's not a dress to live in. To light a fire.

That's why I tore off the dress. In a dream hands don't listen to the head, they don't go where one wants them to, they land somewhere nearby. I still managed to tear the dress off. If it was for special occasions, I didn't want one like this.

That's why I tore the dress off. My dream wasn't changing, though, and if anything changed, it was the weather. I was colder, as if the rain were falling, hard. And wretched, as if nobody was waiting for me anymore.

That's why I tore the dress off.

Ignacy hunched over the oilcloth, over the bouquets for every occasion, rubbed colorless by crockery and dishes, to laughter and to tears, for breakfast and supper. The white and blue bouquet was the most beautiful; right in the center of the oilcloth like a round pretzel. Ignacy hunched over the table: such an old man emerged from him, like a mouse from paste, or a cat out of the bag, or a flour moth. Like the trembling hands of a grandfather from a child, and from the hand—air with feathers, as if a cat had torn a finch apart. Ignacy looked hunched and ancient, one might think he's wise and just.

Sonia sighed, she sighed with hope, as if it wasn't another August passing by, but some September, when the school year began with chances for the new; though Sonia herself hadn't experienced education, one needed the Polish People's Republic for that and it arrived too late—other than her name and surname she had never written anything, perhaps some crosses to indicate she agreed to transfer a field, or for a pension.

Sonia smiled brilliantly at Ignacy, she smiled widely, a porcelain smile. She pulled her hand from her dress. He took the old, stained material, and Sonia placed her hands on her lap.

I lay next to the pitchfork in the ground. I managed to crawl to it, I had no strength for anything else.

I lay there until the end of the world, first as the body, naked, then rotting to the bone, until finally as a piece of field overgrown with roots of weeds.

(Ah, Igor felt touched, Antigone and Polynices! If Sonia were rotting, would anybody bury her?)

It darkened, or maybe it was just dark in front of my eyes. Somebody took me under the arms and began to pull me toward the village. I didn't want it, but how can you not want when your hip is shattered, mouth full of soil, your body empty like a slough without a snake?

I realized by the breathing it was father pulling me. Father breathed like that when he loved me. I knew that breathing and I hated it. More than the beatings.

Father pulled me, like an empty bedsheet duvet case, useless milk, to the hovel. He warmed water, helped me wash and dress. *Paklikali*, a folk healer, who dressed and prayed over my wounds, not for free either. From air and water. A linen sheet and ash in glass. From war and history. Burying the ash at the crossroads and whispering spells: "Who talks of victory? Survive, that is all."

(Rilke? Igor thought, but that might be going too far.)

I didn't expect that father's hands, old and worn, could be so delicate. Could those hands have molded me from mother's body with real love? Did they pick me up and cradle me like the shell does the center of a nut? For the first time this touch didn't burn me like a red-hot iron bar, though my skin was also made of a sheet of tin. Such hands of meat, fingers of bone, couldn't harm me—they couldn't even scratch me.

I lay curled up and under duvets on the *leżajka*. Father lit a lamp on the table, though he was still saving; always a miser,

always in the dark like in the corner of the Orthodox church.
Father looked at me as if I really were his daughter. Father looked
at me as if I really had been created of his loins, and not as if I
were supposed to indulge them.

Father looked at me like a father.

So that's why, I thought, children loved their parents. For that
look. For hands that didn't only punish and hurt, but also healed
the wounds.

"*Heta usio moj hrech,*" father said. "*Ja ciabie pierapraszaju.*"

I lowered my eyelids to indicate yes. Yes, it's your sin, but our
death. It was so easy, list your sins and wait for the leftovers of
forgiveness. So easy, but far from the truth. So easy to let the skin
of my eyelids fall over my eye, like over a bar of soap that slips
from the fingers in a *balejka.*

"*Ty mnie darujesz?*" he asked. "*Ty możasz?*"

I looked at my father. He sat there, *papsawny,* tiny and
unhappy. So unlike father, who loved me in spite of me and in
spite of me he also beat me, walked all over me and hurt me,
pushed himself into me but always backed up in time. Different
people, unlike one another. How to forgive the apologizing one,
the tiny and unhappy one, what the other, big, strong, and cruel,
had done?

Perhaps I could forgive the one that raped and humiliated me,
but I didn't know how to forgive this one, whining for mercy, the
one I didn't know.

"No," I said. "*Ni mahu. Ni chaczu.*"

He was so small, so unhappy, that he only nodded. I pitied
him. But the big and burly one, of veins and muscle, I couldn't
pity, because I couldn't pity that me: small, unhappy, and
trusting. Healthy. That one took what he wanted and now it was
time for me to grab what hurt, but what I didn't need.

"When it reaches me that you're dead, I'll cry for joy," I said,
and that's what I did in the end, in the swamp.

He nodded.

"I'll die happy, because I will know you are crying for joy," he said.

"I only want you to die. Without a grave or a funeral."

The following days, hard as a piece of land, began against my will, they passed and ended against it. I survived thanks to my father's love. I hated him, my hate turned out to be nothing next to his devotion. He fed me, washed me, covered me. He took me out into the woods when the Germans came, and burned a fire day and night. He came running when my breath grew more quiet than the trees, he put his hand on my forehead and murmured prayers. He eventually took my dress from the road.

I owed my life to father, for the second time.

I wanted to die. Not to join Joachim and Mikołaj. Or mother and Witek. I wanted to die to spite father. Not because I didn't have anything to live for. I wanted my father's final effort to end in failure. So he would be left most alone: tiny, shrunken, and alive; alive for a long time.

Loathing, even burning and ironclad, means nothing in the face of love. It drowns like a grain of sand in water, it doesn't float like the dried-cherry pit.

When it became clear that I'd survive, after many days of fever and many nights of falling pinecones, which hit the moss like bombs, when it became clear that I'd survive, I thought that it wasn't fair.

One time, I got whom I wanted—Joachim. And then, like a punishment for getting anyone, piece by piece, person by person, month after month, what I had learned to love was taken away.

Father was the one who told me what happened when I was ill.

The Germans were infuriated by the attack on an SS officer. They prepared for a hunt. They were aware they'd get lost in the woods and the swamp by themselves, so they caught on to a better idea. They handed out weapons to the inhabitants of nearby villages; the war was lost anyway, though it was only blooming, they didn't have to worry how the weapons would be used afterward, against whom; they were more concerned with postwar order. They demanded Misza and Janek's heads. In return they promised to leave the village inhabitants alone. The promise of peace, even broken, was equal to a mountain of gold in times of war. Sonia and her father received the greatest punishment from other villagers: they looked away. For a moment.

It must have been a pitiful hunt. It wasn't really clear who was the prey and who the hunter. Both the prey and the hunter were to lay their heads on the block; it was a matter of time and chance. Did it really matter who killed and why? German, Russian, Belarusian, and Pole shot bullets without nationalities.

Neighbors hunted neighbors.

Misza escaped into the woods. Two from Królowe Stojło found him before two days had passed. Misza shot one, wounded the other; neighbors over the river. It's thanks to the wounded that we know what happened.

Misza shot one. He wasn't even paying attention to the shot. The bullet opened up a third eye in the first one's skull. I hope that he used that newly opened eye to gaze inside himself and see through his remaining two eyes what he was trying to do.

Misza wounded the second one. He wasn't even paying attention to the shot. The bullet shattered the shoulder and stuck fast in a birch trunk. Maybe a pinecone fell, and a spider hung on a thread. Don't kill spiders in a house. It brings bad luck.

Misza walked up to the first, dead one. Then to the second one, writhing in pain, curled like a fallen leaf. And he said:

"Tell them it was me."

He said it and not waiting for any agreement, he put the barrel to his temple.

It's not audible, how the bullet crushes bone and cuts through tissue. The bang is audible, because sound is slower than a bullet, not to mention Witek, my poor, unloved, heavy Witek. A bullet is faster than sound—it enters the body like a nail wood. Like a wedge between the ax head and the handle.

It's not audible, how the bullet crushes bone.

It's not audible, what people think about each other. How they save loved ones in their thoughts. How they pull down the heavens, give up air. How they discover a drooping breast with a drop of milk.

Scene of the Holy Trinity Parabellum.

Pine trees grow from the projector on the empty wood planks of the stage, though birches are also all right if the pine trees are inaccessible, if the white trunks are dimmed. An angel hatches in the sky, hatches from the second projector. This angel is steel gray, the technology is 3D. It has wings bent like a seagull's. The German Junkers Ju 87 had wings like that. And the angel's face is like the pilot's cabin. And its eyes are made of the cabin window's bevels. And its eyes are like a beak or an aerial bomb. Its aureola is a swastika. The choir's sung praises are like the whines of sirens and propellers. And other angels, from the third projector, are like a legion of diving bombers.

The sky grows steel gray, pregnant not with a storm, but fire and dust, and the moan of sirens which draw every listener to their death. To this end of ends leads the hypothesis that there is some God, because there is not justice. Justice is a sin.

On the stage planks, under the dimmed sky, though with blasting engines. Under the ceiling with golden-crystal chandeliers, on the planks there is a stump, and on the stump, Misza. A moment later, two young actors run on. Two shots fall, and after two shots—fall the two actors. Or maybe the actors fall first, and after them—the shots? This isn't a perfect spectacle from a technical point of view.

The images from the projectors lighten gradually. The steel-gray angel is the last to disappear. A third shot sounds, but nothing changes onstage: one actor is sitting, two lie still. Will it now, in the theater, for just one scene, be possible to stop death?

A white background fills Misza's growing face. Unshaven and tired. Wild, but with a shining eye. A barrel to his right temple. To his left, somebody's pale hands, spread and opened upward, like a bowl for nothing, a beggar's.

If an invisible line were stretched from the barrel through Misza's skull, there would be a small tornado at his left temple, attached—like a leech—to the skin. The twister stretches into a funnel shape in a cloud of red droplets and ripped bits of meat and bone, as if someone had sneezed. The eye of this twister, no wider than a pin, is like a kiss sucking the bone marrow from the bones, also from hunger.

And so ends Misza, Sonia's husband, keeper of her lie and protector of her belly. So he ends. In his own wood and by his own hand. A stolen weapon, a life snatched out of history's throat prematurely. The life escaped in a pocket-twister of blood drops and ripped bits of meat and bone.

Before he falls, he'll remember the most beautiful moments of his life, that's the convention of death. Icons darkened by candlelight in gilded frames and Sonia at the cemetery, when she said, "I'm with you," though he didn't hear it then. He didn't hear it then but he does now, as if the bells in the bell tower had finally learned to speak, not threaten with hell or fire.

And then he will fall on the moss. Moss is soft. First, Misza will sink into the forest cover, then the crows will descend to feast on his eyes, then wild dogs and wolves will nibble on the gamy meat, and a magpie will take the wedding ring for its nest. Pure gold, the most difficult challenge, over the heads of the mushroom pickers, under the black tail, in its claws or beak, straight to the next, in which nobody eats gold or vows forever.

Many years later, not that long ago, over many hills and swamps, over many reforms, over many dark goals and many lies signed with a cross because the fingers were broken, and letters not taught, many years later Sonia went to pick blueberries, she went many times. And what happened once is that she got lost.

Tired, she sat on a felled tree. The rotten trunk cracked, and Sonia fell on her back, for the second time. And then she looked under the turf, revealed after many years. She saw a few bones of a hand. The bones were wrapped tightly over a handgun. The handgun was covered with rust, the bones with a purple mold. Sonia spat, then she crossed herself thrice. She got up and found the path home.

Coincidences like that don't happen to respectable people, only cursed ones, marked with a cross.

Sonia finished talking about Misza. Misza pulled the trigger again. He went to hell again, or some other place, wherever suicides are led to down paths lined with priests and dogmas. Wherever they go, it cannot be a good place, because life was hopeless, and death only slightly gentler. Sonia imagined such a place as a plain—a flat sky and flat land, emptiness in which the line of the horizon is the only thing that exists. A line, a clean slice of the scissors, when hope has been detached without frayed ends or threads.

Sońka lies on the *leżajka*, Ignacy is by the kitchen table, Igor is watchful, always at work, always making his career, everything might be useful, he recycles pain and death. The only death left to be told was Janek's.

There isn't much to say. They killed him two weeks later. I think ours did the killing, because they let me live. Their consciences were so burdened that they left me alive. Or maybe they have no consciences? History is evil. An evil as big as *Haspodź* himself. Evil that doesn't exist, yet simultaneously destroys.

Ignacy thought that Sonia should wear the dress with blue flowers and a mottled stain, the dress from once upon a time. The coda dress. The ripped and stained dress—like the twentieth century. But Sonia was sitting in an ordinary dark caftan, and he was squeezing the bundle with the dress.

Sonia lifted her head delicately and stood up.

"It's time for me," she said. "Nobody's waiting."

She drank a little water. The curtain fell, a fifteen-minute interval, the toilet invites, follow the green arrows, Toilet, not Exit.

Sonia straightened the caftan's material. Jozik meowed. She touched Ignacy's face with a hand of parchment, and Igor flinched. She took her shawl off. She tied her white hair into a ponytail with a band. She walked into the small bedroom, which led to the guest room. In the bedroom, next to the bed and icon, there was a wooden table, and on it a black-and-white television set. The table was unstable, and the television broke three years ago. The last image it showed was a snowstorm.

Sonia walked through the bedroom and lay on the neatly made bed in the guest room, in the *wielkaj chaci*. She never slept here. Today, she felt like a guest, a guest in her home and in the world. The duvets and pillows didn't even bend. She crossed herself and crossed her arms on her chest. She closed her eyes and that's all she saw of the earth—the planks of the ceiling with a spiderweb in the corner. Spiders in the house bring luck. Don't kill, you're at war!

I didn't finish listening, he thought, just one more breath, I'm not allowed not to hear it. He leaned down, to stroke the cat. The cat didn't move. It was frozen in death, like source documents.

Daylight in the kitchen. Sonia is dead. Only two people know this: she and Igor. He opened the cupboard door—*chlapauki*, because the doors make a hlap-hlap sound—to make sure that the teeth are on a napkin. They are. White, from chinaware. With the pink meat of plastic gums.

On the tin sheet, near the logs, lies the cat. It's as stiff as a wooden figure. Molted fur, there is more dust on it than stripes. The ninth body of Jozik the Mouse Shepherd.

He never started a fire. Now he put in thinner and thinner logs. He'd be quicker at starting a flood than a fire.

He sat next to Sonia on the bed. He could have grabbed her hand, like in a movie, but there was nobody watching them, he just sat next to her, on the chair, with his hands on his knees. His palms first opened upward, like during yoga, but as soon as he realized this he fixed their position so they were neutral in symbolic terms, empty.

He wasn't gazing at Sonia at all, that would be rude, invasive. He'll look as soon as she's gone, when she walks out. He waited for the final breath.

He heard it.

He heard the final breath.

It was louder, underscored by a silky moan. And after it a series of sounds resembling delicate blowing on something hot, almost soundless, but there was no life in them. Puff, puff. This body, just the body, abandoned by its owner, was making space in itself for death, for bugs and rot. Now it was its own, its own self, Sońka would say, that is, nobody's.

He should start to organize her death. She had nobody. She met only those who organized her life, and not a single person from death.

When he thought that he could just walk out and trust decay, as if they had never met, he felt such terror that he felt breathless.

Electricity ran through him, a strong hit, blue lightning.

Then he heard mooing. It was Mućka.

Yes. Sońka would have to wait her turn. The cow had to be milked first. He hoped this would turn out to be simpler than lighting a fire.

He went out into the yard. Light again.

And Borbus curled up under the bench.

He didn't have to check. He knew that it would be stiff, or maybe only a little warm.

Someone turn the sun already.

Sonia crossed her hands on her chest. She died as one should—respectably, in the early hours and amen.

Sonia's funeral was a rather modest, if costly, affair, like her life. There weren't many guests. Królowe Stojło and Słuczanka, a few people from Gródek, Walił, and Zarzeczan. There weren't many guests, though the wreaths were enormous. Igor planted Sonia's final path with a sea of flowers, an ocean and wave and turbulent waters, for lots of money.

And the most stunning wreath, as if taken straight from the oilcloth, looked like this: round and as huge as a tractor's back wheel; wreathed from goose feathers as white as a first snow, pulled to redness close to the quill, to the honking of geese and the snake-like movements of their necks, and between the feathers forget-me-nots were placed, tiny blue petals with a yellow eye, and the sash of Sonia's dress, and on the sash golden letters and mottled stains of blood were embroidered. A sign with pathos: "I'm with you." Who said it to whom? Igor to Ignacy? Ignacy to Sonia? Sonia to Misza? Theater to life? Life to art? Blame to respectability?

This wreath was like a giant eye, like a cataract, like a final sight of land, and in the middle there was nothing, like a blind spot of life. Because of this nothing, when the wreath was carried, trees and the funeral procession shone through, and when one tripped—sky, for a moment, at most two—three steps, and then—freshly moved earth.

It was the most beautiful and pretentious wreath that had ever been placed at the cemetery in Gródek. Sonia probably wouldn't have liked it. Although perhaps she would have?

The light changed to golden green. Sonia lay on the evenly made bed. The duvets and pillows didn't even bend; in the theater they were made of hard foam. The duvets and pillows didn't even bend. She crossed herself and crossed her arms on her chest. She closed her eyes and that's all she saw of earth—the planks of the ceiling with a spiderweb in the corner.

Spiders in the house bring luck. Don't kill! So the sixth, only the sixth, commandment, in a pre-Christian engraving. Don't kill is sixth, remember and count on the fingers of one hand. Reach your own conclusions, otherwise the same thing will happen that didn't fit on the fingers so many times before.

Ignacy followed in Sonia's footsteps to the guest room.

She was lying with her hands already crossed on her chest. Younger than a few hours previously, as young as when her life was gambled away, though she hadn't gambled at all, she placed no bets and expected no rewards. Her body was filled with darkness: juices, lust, devotion. Peace and calm. Waiting. The pair of old geezers: Eros and Thanatos.

"*Pryniasi serca*," Sonia asked.

Ignacy didn't understand at first. The actor pauses at this point, now still onstage. And then the actor goes offstage, to the kitchen, and returns with chocolates. Sonia smiles, toothless. She hugs the box and places the heart where it should be; between the breasts, visible, honest, and paid for.

"Take me across," Sonia said.

Ignacy hesitates. Borbus the Twelfth howls outside. It's not a pitiful howl. It was a knowing howl, like a coin that opened more and more gates. Borbus howled with the whole force of her lungs and canine love, from the awful bits of hair on her back. Her howl rose up to cloud nine and fell down to the Twelfth Circle.

It was a howl of the heralds. It was elicited from a dog's throat, but it might as well have come from one of the gold mines of Abyssinia. It was a howl to celebrate a happy ending. A howl of the last stanza, light and cheerful, ignoring the sad stanzas of Dante and Shakespeare. A howl to celebrate ordinary death, the foundation of civilization.

Sonia the White and Sonia the Broken. Sonia longhaired and long-living. With the big heart and baby gums. Sonia, who cast curses on the cows of her enemies and good spells on the women of her adversaries.

"*Pierawedzi*," she repeated.

Ignacy hesitated.

The actor froze, waiting.

Borbus the Last howled. She howled for the first father, the one with the spiky ears and soft fur, the one on the cloud and on top of Mount Tabor.

How happy my paws are, leaping and running. How happy my teeth are, carrying sticks in a game of fetch. How happy my fur is, being brushed free of fleas. My mistress, Sonia, has begun her journey. And I bark and bark, chasing chickens and licking her calves. Soon we will enter the blue doghouse and they will give us golden chains, endless chains. We will be tied up outside of time, my mistress and I, forever and until never.

Ignacy put his hand on Sonia's forehead.

The actor bows, as if he were in front of an iconostasis. He crossed himself in the Orthodox way, against the grain of the Catholic cross, like a reflection, with nothing in between, an optical illusion. Sonia's forehead resembled a boat, and his hand was an oar, and there was no Jonas inside, no surprise, and nothing for free.

He tried to remember some prayers. *Krinomenos*—being judged. Only that came to mind, and not because he was a believer, but because he remembered from his time at university.

He swallowed. It was more difficult to say goodbye than it was to greet someone, he thought. It was harder to help someone across than it was to ask them to leave. How smoothly it goes.

I, Igor, heard how Ignacy, during the many murderous rehearsals, swallowed loudly in the guest room. I heard the howling of the dog, which was joined by the meows of Jozik the Mouseherd. I heard the sentences uttered by the speakers of the laptop. A recording of the sound check.

Ignacy could not recall any appropriate words or routines. Because the fat Polish bishops are a joke, as are the bearded Orthodox priests. I had to help him, help myself.

And everything has to work onstage. It has to touch. Tug at the heartstrings. Make breathing difficult. Preferably in black and white, then you know it's Important and Timeless. Nobody can see now, but everyone will later. And that will be embarrassing.

Only an unfamiliar word came to mind—Kaddish: a great scenographic risk, a threat, like dragging up the Holocaust again. Tacky. But without it, the show probably won't work. And does it really matter, what touches people? A masterpiece or a tacky story? The "being touched" is the same either way.

(Do Jews have catharsis—Igor wondered—and if not, do they borrow it from the Greeks when they need it? Is that what it's like, those who don't have borrowing from those who do?)

There is nothing closer to the heart than alienation or difference. Kaddish Yatom, Kaddish of orphans, said by the son of a dead woman, every day for eleven months. We practically became her children, Sonia's children, pulled suddenly out of a hat, by the ears like you'd pull a rabbit, just before her death. Death was on our side, and on Sonia's, it was our ally. It was a reassuring rule, a promise that "after" there really was nothing. Nothing. There is nothing. Fear not.

I rise from the armchair, not feeling much pain, only anger at the actor playing Ignacy, he's making a scene, he must have spent too much time in school plays. I was at the edge of the stage in a matter of steps.

Ignacy's hand runs over Sonia's forehead. His hand is brittle, like our faith: you won't find an end to the search, or a beginning, you won't find anything in the time after life.

"*Jitgadal wejitkadasz szemech raba,*" he says, because he memorized it, and I, following him onstage, respond unconsciously: *Amen.*

Now the light is dimming—maybe some music? Arvo Pärt? Though I'm not convinced—a spotlight of bittersweetness on Sonia's bed.

Bealema di wera chirutech. Wejamlich malchuteh bechajeichon uwejomeichon uwechajei dechol beit Jisrael baagala uwizman kariw. Weimru: Amen.

We say: *Amen.*

Jozik rubs himself against my legs. Borbus the Last arrives, flea-bitten and graying on the muzzle.

Jehe szemeh raba mewarach lealam ulealemei alemaja. Jitbarach wejisztabach wejitpaar wejitromam wejitnase wejithadar wejitale wejithalal szemeh dekudsza berich hu.

We reply: *Berich hu.*

We reply: He who is blessed.

And I feel something strange on my skin, in my groin, everywhere, like ant bites: as if I were being told as well as if I were telling.

Leela min kol birchata weszirata tuszbeta wenechemata daamiran bealema. Weimru: Amen.

We reply: *Amen.*

Misza has come, the understudy, because the actor has caught some infection. The carpet doesn't dent, the wood doesn't squeak, the hole on the head isn't gaping, only Borbus looks happy.

Jehe szelama raba min szemaja, wechajim aleinu weal kol Jisrael. Weimru: Amen.

We reply: *Amen*, while Ignacy takes three steps back, steps that have not been approved by the director and are outside of the play. His hand leaves Sonia's forehead and his lungs take in air, as if he wanted to blow wind into the sails of a ship, or use the breath to greet his grandparents. Push a boat across the final body of water.

And I can feel a stranger behind me. A bright man, straight from Sonia's memory. Straight as a tail on a falling star. So he too has come, the Central American planter and SS officer, the bright Joachim, the scratch on heaven and skin?

Witek is here too. And Janek.

Ose szalom bimromaw, hu jaase szalom aleinu, weal kol Jisrael. Weimru: Amen.

Only one person is missing from the group we need to create the prayer circle. To finally say goodbye to history, our sworn enemy. *Minjan.* Nine. Someone is missing.

Perhaps it is you we need?

More than we know how to say?

In the dance of bodies and shadows?

You?

"*Heta usio ni majo, zusim,*" said Sonia.

He wondered how to use the Milky Way to make butter.
He'd had no success with the cows
Tymoteusz Karpowicz
Małe cienie wielkich czarnoksiężników

Any resemblance to real people, places, events, and the Second World War is intended, and also completely unauthorized.

Belarusian Dictionary

Hospadzi—God/Lord

Nu, Mućka, paszła.—Come on, Mućka, go.

kaluczki—small fish living in streams and rivers

Tfu, prystanuli i buduć scać.—Tfu, they stopped and are going to piss.

zdychlina—corpse

Spasi, Hospadzi, spasi.—Save us, Lord, save us.

Musi jaki durak, bez struka.—Probably some idiot, without a penis.

Dobry dzień, szto stałaso?—Good day, has something happened?

kastrule—pots

Mućka, nastupisa, bladzina.—Mućka, move over, pale one.

Chadzi na małako, chadzi.—Come for milk, come.

leżajka—part of a kitchen tiled stove, used to sit or lie on, found in country houses and towns in Podlasie

baciuszka—Orthodox priest

Wy, Sońka, zdureli.—You, Sońka, have gone stupid.

szmatnik—a welcome mat woven on a loom from material from old clothes cut into stripes

Patom razpalu u pieczy.—I'll light the fire later.

Dzicia lubi jak duszu, a trasi jak hruszu.—Love the child like your own soul, and shake it like a pear tree.

muszczyna—a man

Ihar—Igor

Na, pahladzi.—Here, look.

Heta jaho krou.—That's his blood.

żywina—farm animals

Pa noczy tolki katy i bladzi łaziać.—At night, only cats and sluts walk.

A ty majesz krou na rukach.—You have blood on your hands.

139

Laży, ja raskażu.—Lie still, I will tell.

taukanica—cooked and mashed potatoes, baked on the oven slab

plita—the oven slab

Skol heta barachło?—Where is this useless old stuff from?

wiły—pitchfork

krapiwa—nettles

Wieruju wo jediniho Boha Otca.—I believe in one God the Father.

Skaży, jak można palubić tak druhoho czaławieka? Czamu? Pa szto?—Tell me, how can you love another person so much? Why? For what?

Ty ni swaja. Ty bladź.—You're not one of us. You're a slut.

Ciapier srać ni budziasz, job twaju mać.—You won't shit now, fuck your mother.

Lapiej pamirać u łóżku, u swajoj chaci. U szpitalu feko.—It's better to die in bed in your own home. It's bad in the hosptial.

trasianka—a specific mixture of Russian and Belarusian

mużyk—man

Ty kurwa, mnie ustydna.—You slut, I'm ashamed.

słonczyk—a low stool

Ihnat—Ignacy

Trzymajcia dobra.—Hold tight.

Heta czyj bastruk?—Whose bastard is that?

Nałhała ja.—I lied.

Idzi papratać, a ty paklicz na wieczar Wańka z Miszaj.—Go clean up, and you invite Wańka and Misza for tonight.

Znajasz, Wańka, maju doczku, Sońku?—Do you, Wańka, know my daughter, Sońka?

Znaju. Jana udana wielmi, wykapana Gala.—I know her. She turned out well, the image of Gala.

Jana ni feka, tolki szto ja tabie skażu sztoś wielmi śmiesznaho. Sońka, chadzi siudy, padydzi, docześka.—She's not bad,

but I'll tell you something really funny. Sońka, come
here, come closer, daughter.

Ty hladzi, jana panna, a z żywatom jak żonka.—Look, a maiden,
but with a belly like a wife.

Żywot ni uziałsa z pawietra. Żywot Sońki uziałsa z Miszy.—The
belly didn't come from the air. It came from Misza.

hadaść—disgusting; here: snakes, lizards

Heta prauda. My ni znali, jak wam skazać. Ustydna było.—It's
true. We didn't know how to tell you. We were ashamed.

Heta ni moża być.—It can't be.

lelak—simpleton, pushover

Chaczu paczakać.—I want to wait.

u buchtu, w pizdu—here: for nothing

lizun—a kind of snowy embankment

bulwa—potato

pakrowa—an icon of Mary, but also the Intercession of the The
otokos

Ja prapała. Prapała.—I'm lost. Lost.

Czamu ty mnie uział, czamu?—Why did you take me, why?

Jon wiarnułsa. Jon wiarnułsa znou.—He's back. He's back again.

paklikali—they called

Heta usio moj hrech. Ja ciabie pierapraszaju.—It's all my sin. I'm
sorry.

balejka—tub

Ty mnie darujesz? Ty możasz?—Will you forgive me? Can you?

papsawny—broken

Ni mahu. Ni chaczu.—I can't. I don't want to.

w wielkaj chaci—in the big room

chlapauka—a dresser with cupboards

Pryniasi serca.—Bring the hearts.

pierawiedzi—take me through

Heta usio ni majo, zusim.—It's all not mine, not at all.

IGNACY KARPOWICZ is a Polish writer and translator. His fifth work, *Balladyny i romanse*, won him the Polityka Passport Prize in 2010. He was previously nominated for this award for his debut novel, *Niehalo* (2006), and has since been nominated for the Nike Literary Award for *Gesty* (2009), *Balladyny i romanse* (2011), *osci* (2013), and *Sońka* (2015).

MAYA ZAKRZEWSKA-PIM is a Polish-British translator. She grew up and lived in Warsaw before studying English at Trinity College, Dublin. She completed an MPhil in Education at the University of Cambridge, and is currently studying for a PhD. Ignacy Karpowicz's *Sońka* is her second published translation.

MICHAL AJVAZ, *The Golden Age.*
The Other City.
PIERRE ALBERT-BIROT, *Grabinoulor.*
YUZ ALESHKOVSKY, *Kangaroo.*
SVETLANA ALEXIEVICH, *Voices from Chernobyl.*
FELIPE ALFAU, *Chromos.*
Locos.
JOAO ALMINO, *Enigmas of Spring.*
IVAN ÂNGELO, *The Celebration.*
The Tower of Glass.
ANTÓNIO LOBO ANTUNES, *Knowledge of Hell.*
The Splendor of Portugal.
ALAIN ARIAS-MISSON, *Theatre of Incest.*
JOHN ASHBERY & JAMES SCHUYLER, *A Nest of Ninnies.*
GABRIELA AVIGUR-ROTEM, *Heatwave and Crazy Birds.*
DJUNA BARNES, *Ladies Almanack.*
Ryder.
JOHN BARTH, *Letters.*
Sabbatical.
Collected Stories.
DONALD BARTHELME, *The King.*
Paradise.
SVETISLAV BASARA, *Chinese Letter.*
Fata Morgana.
In Search of the Grail.
MIQUEL BAUÇÀ, *The Siege in the Room.*
RENÉ BELLETTO, *Dying.*
MAREK BIENCZYK, *Transparency.*
ANDREI BITOV, *Pushkin House.*
ANDREJ BLATNIK, *You Do Understand.*
Law of Desire.
LOUIS PAUL BOON, *Chapel Road.*
My Little War.
Summer in Termuren.
ROGER BOYLAN, *Killoyle.*
IGNÁCIO DE LOYOLA BRANDÃO, *Anonymous Celebrity.*
Zero.
BRIGID BROPHY, *In Transit.*
The Prancing Novelist.

GABRIELLE BURTON, *Heartbreak Hotel.*
MICHEL BUTOR, *Degrees.*
Mobile.
G. CABRERA INFANTE, *Infante's Inferno.*
Three Trapped Tigers.
JULIETA CAMPOS, *The Fear of Losing Eurydice.*
ANNE CARSON, *Eros the Bittersweet.*
ORLY CASTEL-BLOOM, *Dolly City.*
LOUIS-FERDINAND CÉLINE, *North.*
Conversations with Professor Y.
London Bridge.
HUGO CHARTERIS, *The Tide Is Right.*
ERIC CHEVILLARD, *Demolishing Nisard.*
The Author and Me.
MARC CHOLODENKO, *Mordechai Schamz.*
EMILY HOLMES COLEMAN, *The Shutter of Snow.*
ERIC CHEVILLARD, *The Author and Me.*
LUIS CHITARRONI, *The No Variations.*
CH'OE YUN, *Mannequin.*
ROBERT COOVER, *A Night at the Movies.*
STANLEY CRAWFORD, *Log of the S.S.*
The Mrs Unguentine.
Some Instructions to My Wife.
RALPH CUSACK, *Cadenza.*
NICHOLAS DELBANCO, *Sherbrookes.*
The Count of Concord.
NIGEL DENNIS, *Cards of Identity.*
PETER DIMOCK, *A Short Rhetoric for Leaving the Family.*
ARIEL DORFMAN, *Konfidenz.*
COLEMAN DOWELL, *Island People.*
Too Much Flesh and Jabez.
RIKKI DUCORNET, *Phosphor in Dreamland.*
The Complete Butcher's Tales.
RIKKI DUCORNET (cont.), *The Jade Cabinet.*
The Fountains of Neptune.
WILLIAM EASTLAKE, *Castle Keep.*
Lyric of the Circle Heart.
JEAN ECHENOZ, *Chopin's Move.*

FOR A FULL LIST OF PUBLICATIONS, VISIT: www.dalkeyarchive.com

STANLEY ELKIN, *A Bad Man.*
The Dick Gibson Show.
The Franchiser.
FRANÇOIS EMMANUEL, *Invitation to a Voyage.*
SALVADOR ESPRIU, *Ariadne in the Grotesque Labyrinth.*
LESLIE A. FIEDLER, *Love and Death in the American Novel.*
JUAN FILLOY, *Op Oloop.*
GUSTAVE FLAUBERT, *Bouvard and Pécuchet.*
JON FOSSE, *Aliss at the Fire.*
Melancholy.
Trilogy.
FORD MADOX FORD, *The March of Literature.*
MAX FRISCH, *I'm Not Stiller.*
Man in the Holocene.
CARLOS FUENTES, *Christopher Unborn.*
Distant Relations.
Terra Nostra.
Where the Air Is Clear.
Nietzsche on His Balcony.
WILLIAM GADDIS, JR., *The Recognitions.*
JR.
JANICE GALLOWAY, *Foreign Parts.*
The Trick Is to Keep Breathing.
WILLIAM H. GASS, *Life Sentences.*
The Tunnel.
The World Within the Word.
Willie Masters' Lonesome Wife.
GÉRARD GAVARRY, *Hoppla! 1 2 3.*
ETIENNE GILSON, *The Arts of the Beautiful.*
Forms and Substances in the Arts.
C. S. GISCOMBE, *Giscome Road.*
Here.
DOUGLAS GLOVER, *Bad News of the Heart.*
WITOLD GOMBROWICZ, *A Kind of Testament.*
PAULO EMÍLIO SALES GOMES, *P's Three Women.*
GEORGI GOSPODINOV, *Natural Novel.*

JUAN GOYTISOLO, *Juan the Landless.*
Makbara.
Marks of Identity.
JACK GREEN, *Fire the Bastards!*
JIŘÍ GRUŠA, *The Questionnaire.*
MELA HARTWIG, *Am I a Redundant Human Being?*
JOHN HAWKES, *The Passion Artist.*
Whistlejacket.
ELIZABETH HEIGHWAY, ED., *Contemporary Georgian Fiction.*
AIDAN HIGGINS, *Balcony of Europe.*
Blind Man's Bluff.
Bornholm Night-Ferry.
Langrishe, Go Down.
Scenes from a Receding Past.
ALDOUS HUXLEY, *Antic Hay.*
Point Counter Point.
Those Barren Leaves.
Time Must Have a Stop.
JANG JUNG-IL, *When Adam Opens His Eyes*
DRAGO JANČAR, *The Tree with No Name.*
I Saw Her That Night.
Galley Slave.
MIKHEIL JAVAKHISHVILI, *Kvachi.*
GERT JONKE, *The Distant Sound.*
Homage to Czerny.
The System of Vienna.
JACQUES JOUET, *Mountain R.*
Savage.
Upstaged.
JUNG YOUNG-MOON, *A Contrived World.*
MIEKO KANAI, *The Word Book.*
YORAM KANIUK, *Life on Sandpaper.*
ZURAB KARUMIDZE, *Dagny.*
PABLO KATCHADJIAN, *What to Do.*
JOHN KELLY, *From Out of the City.*
HUGH KENNER, *Flaubert, Joyce and Beckett: The Stoic Comedians.*
Joyce's Voices.
DANILO KIŠ, *The Attic.*
The Lute and the Scars.
Psalm 44.
A Tomb for Boris Davidovich.
ANITA KONKKA, *A Fool's Paradise.*

GEORGE KONRÁD, *The City Builder.*
TADEUSZ KONWICKI, *A Minor Apocalypse.*
The Polish Complex.
ELAINE KRAF, *The Princess of 72nd Street.*
JIM KRUSOE, *Iceland.*
AYSE KULIN, *Farewell: A Mansion in Occupied Istanbul.*
EMILIO LASCANO TEGUI, *On Elegance While Sleeping.*
ERIC LAURRENT, *Do Not Touch.*
VIOLETTE LEDUC, *La Bâtarde.*
LEE KI-HO, *At Least We Can Apologize.*
EDOUARD LEVÉ, *Autoportrait.*
Suicide.
MARIO LEVI, *Istanbul Was a Fairy Tale.*
DEBORAH LEVY, *Billy and Girl.*
JOSÉ LEZAMA LIMA, *Paradiso.*
OSMAN LINS, *Avalovara.*
The Queen of the Prisons of Greece.
ALF MACLOCHLAINN, *Out of Focus.*
Past Habitual.
RON LOEWINSOHN, *Magnetic Field(s).*
YURI LOTMAN, *Non-Memoirs.*
D. KEITH MANO, *Take Five.*
MINA LOY, *Stories and Essays of Mina Loy.*
MICHELINE AHARONIAN MARCOM, *The Mirror in the Well.*
BEN MARCUS, *The Age of Wire and String.*
WALLACE MARKFIELD, *Teitlebaum's Window.*
To an Early Grave.
DAVID MARKSON, *Reader's Block.*
Wittgenstein's Mistress.
CAROLE MASO, *AVA.*
HISAKI MATSUURA, *Triangle.*
LADISLAV MATEJKA & KRYSTYNA POMORSKA, EDS., *Readings in Russian Poetics: Formalist & Structuralist Views.*
HARRY MATHEWS, *Cigarettes.*
The Conversions.
The Human Country.
The Journalist.
My Life in CIA.

Singular Pleasures.
The Sinking of the Odradek.
Stadium.
Tlooth.
JOSEPH MCELROY, *Night Soul and Other Stories.*
ABDELWAHAB MEDDEB, *Talismano.*
GERHARD MEIER, *Isle of the Dead.*
HERMAN MELVILLE, *The Confidence-Man.*
AMANDA MICHALOPOULOU, *I'd Like.*
STEVEN MILLHAUSER, *The Barnum Museum.*
In the Penny Arcade.
RALPH J. MILLS, JR., *Essays on Poetry.*
CHRISTINE MONTALBETTI, *The Origin of Man.*
Western.
NICHOLAS MOSLEY, *Accident.*
Assassins.
Catastrophe Practice.
Hopeful Monsters.
Imago Bird.
Natalie Natalia.
Serpent.
WARREN MOTTE, *Fiction Now: The French Novel in the 21st Century.*
Oulipo: A Primer of Potential Literature.
GERALD MURNANE, *Barley Patch.*
Inland.
YVES NAVARRE, *Our Share of Time.*
Sweet Tooth.
DOROTHY NELSON, *In Night's City.*
Tar and Feathers.
WILFRIDO D. NOLLEDO, *But for the Lovers.*
BORIS A. NOVAK, *The Master of Insomnia.*
FLANN O'BRIEN, *At Swim-Two-Birds.*
The Best of Myles.
The Dalkey Archive.
The Hard Life.
The Poor Mouth.
The Third Policeman.
CLAUDE OLLIER, *The Mise-en-Scène.*
Wert and the Life Without End.

PATRIK OUŘEDNÍK, *Europeana.*
The Opportune Moment, 1855.
BORIS PAHOR, *Necropolis.*
FERNANDO DEL PASO, *News from the Empire.*
Palinuro of Mexico.
ROBERT PINGET, *The Inquisitory.*
Mahu or The Material.
Trio.
MANUEL PUIG, *Betrayed by Rita Hayworth.*
The Buenos Aires Affair.
Heartbreak Tango.
RAYMOND QUENEAU, *The Last Days.*
Odile.
Pierrot Mon Ami.
Saint Glinglin.
ANN QUIN, *Berg.*
Passages.
Three.
Tripticks.
ISHMAEL REED, *The Free-Lance Pallbearers.*
The Last Days of Louisiana Red.
Ishmael Reed: The Plays.
Juice!
The Terrible Threes.
The Terrible Twos.
Yellow Back Radio Broke-Down.
RAINER MARIA RILKE,
The Notebooks of Malte Laurids Brigge.
JULIÁN RÍOS, *The House of Ulysses.*
Larva: A Midsummer Night's Babel.
Poundemonium.
ALAIN ROBBE-GRILLET, *Project for a Revolution in New York.*
A Sentimental Novel.
AUGUSTO ROA BASTOS, *I the Supreme.*
DANIËL ROBBERECHTS, *Arriving in Avignon.*
JEAN ROLIN, *The Explosion of the Radiator Hose.*
OLIVIER ROLIN, *Hotel Crystal.*
ALIX CLEO ROUBAUD, *Alix's Journal.*
JACQUES ROUBAUD, *The Form of a City Changes Faster, Alas, Than the Human Heart.*

The Great Fire of London.
Hortense in Exile.
Hortense Is Abducted.
Mathematics: The Plurality of Worlds of Lewis.
Some Thing Black.
RAYMOND ROUSSEL, *Impressions of Africa.*
VEDRANA RUDAN, *Night.*
GERMAN SADULAEV, *The Maya Pill.*
TOMAŽ ŠALAMUN, *Soy Realidad.*
LYDIE SALVAYRE, *The Company of Ghosts.*
LUIS RAFAEL SÁNCHEZ, *Macho Camacho's Beat.*
SEVERO SARDUY, *Cobra & Maitreya.*
NATHALIE SARRAUTE, *Do You Hear Them?*
Martereau.
The Planetarium.
STIG SÆTERBAKKEN, *Siamese.*
Self-Control.
Through the Night.
ARNO SCHMIDT, *Collected Novellas.*
Collected Stories.
Nobodaddy's Children.
Two Novels.
ASAF SCHURR, *Motti.*
GAIL SCOTT, *My Paris.*
JUNE AKERS SEESE,
Is This What Other Women Feel Too?
BERNARD SHARE, *Inish.*
Transit.
VIKTOR SHKLOVSKY, *Bowstring.*
Literature and Cinematography.
Theory of Prose.
Third Factory.
Zoo, or Letters Not about Love.
PIERRE SINIAC, *The Collaborators.*
KJERSTI A. SKOMSVOLD,
The Faster I Walk, the Smaller I Am.
JOSEF ŠKVORECKÝ, *The Engineer of Human Souls.*
GILBERT SORRENTINO, *Aberration of Starlight.*
Blue Pastoral.
Crystal Vision.

Imaginative Qualities of Actual Things.
Mulligan Stew.
Red the Fiend.
Steelwork.
Under the Shadow.
ANDRZEJ STASIUK, *Dukla.*
Fado.
GERTRUDE STEIN, *The Making of Americans.*
A Novel of Thank You.
PIOTR SZEWC, *Annihilation.*
GONÇALO M. TAVARES, *A Man: Klaus Klump.*
Jerusalem.
Learning to Pray in the Age of Technique.
LUCIAN DAN TEODOROVICI, *Our Circus Presents...*
NIKANOR TERATOLOGEN, *Assisted Living.*
STEFAN THEMERSON, *Hobson's Island.*
The Mystery of the Sardine.
Tom Harris.
JOHN TOOMEY, *Sleepwalker.*
Huddleston Road.
Slipping.
DUMITRU TSEPENEAG, *Hotel Europa.*
The Necessary Marriage.
Pigeon Post.
Vain Art of the Fugue.
La Belle Roumaine.
Waiting: Stories.
ESTHER TUSQUETS, *Stranded.*
DUBRAVKA UGRESIC, *Lend Me Your Character.*
Thank You for Not Reading.
TOR ULVEN, *Replacement.*
MATI UNT, *Brecht at Night.*
Diary of a Blood Donor.
Things in the Night.
ÁLVARO URIBE & OLIVIA SEARS, EDS., *Best of Contemporary Mexican Fiction.*
ELOY URROZ, *Friction.*
The Obstacles.
LUISA VALENZUELA, *Dark Desires and the Others.*
He Who Searches.

PAUL VERHAEGHEN, *Omega Minor.*
BORIS VIAN, *Heartsnatcher.*
TOOMAS VINT, *An Unending Landscape.*
ORNELA VORPSI, *The Country Where No One Ever Dies.*
AUSTRYN WAINHOUSE, *Hedyphagetica.*
MARKUS WERNER, *Cold Shoulder.*
Zundel's Exit.
CURTIS WHITE, *The Idea of Home.*
Memories of My Father Watching TV.
Requiem.
DIANE WILLIAMS, *Excitability: Selected Stories.*
DOUGLAS WOOLF, *Wall to Wall.*
Ya! & John-Juan.
JAY WRIGHT, *Polynomials and Pollen.*
The Presentable Art of Reading Absence.
PHILIP WYLIE, *Generation of Vipers.*
MARGUERITE YOUNG, *Angel in the Forest.*
Miss MacIntosh, My Darling.
REYOUNG, *Unbabbling.*
ZORAN ŽIVKOVIĆ, *Hidden Camera.*
LOUIS ZUKOFSKY, *Collected Fiction.*
VITOMIL ZUPAN, *Minuet for Guitar.*
SCOTT ZWIREN, *God Head.*

AND MORE...